NINE MONTHS

Candace

by Maggie Wells

E

EPIC
Press

Candace
Nine Months: Book #1

Written by Maggie Wells

Copyright © 2016 by Abdo Consulting Group, Inc.

Published by EPIC Press™
PO Box 398166
Minneapolis, MN 55439

Cover design by Candice Keimig
Images for cover art obtained from iStockPhoto.com
Edited by Lisa Owens

LIBRARY OF CONGRESS CATALOGING-IN-PUBLICATION DATA

Wells, Maggie.
Candace / Maggie Wells.
p. cm. — (Nine months; #1)
Summary: Candace, a 17-year-old high school senior, is a smart girl who attends an
elite prep school and is on her way to Princeton. She hopes her walk on the wild side
will both punish and attract the attention of her very absent parents when she finds
herself pregnant. Faced with the reality of leaving her innocence, Candace struggles
to choose the right path—motherhood or the Ivy League?
ISBN 978-1-68076-190-0 (hardcover)
1. Teenagers—Sexual behavior—Fiction. 2. Teenage pregnancy—Fiction. 3. High
schools—Fiction. 4. Sex—Fiction. 5. Young adult fiction. I. Title.
[Fic]—dc23
2015949409

To my literary guiding light, Lewis Buzbee

One

It was finals week in December of Candace's senior year. Everyone was packing and leaving. Cars and shuttle buses were coming and going to the airport, bus station, train station. Candace sat on her bed and watched her roommate, Molly, stuff every last designer sweater and pair of jeans into her suitcase.

"Got any big plans for Christmas break?" Molly asked.

"Hang out with the 'rents in Boston. You?" Candace said.

"We're going skiing in Switzerland," Molly said. "You should come."

"Who is we?"

"Brett, Perry, Eric, the gang. Jude's step-dad rented a place in Zermatt."

"Too bad. Wish I had more notice," said Candace, knowing that she couldn't afford a ski trip to Switzerland.

"Should be fun, kid. See you next year." Molly dragged her massive bag out into the hallway.

Candace was not like the other kids at St. Paul's Boarding School in Concord, New Hampshire. She called them "Paulies" and "Paulines," the ones whose fathers were investment bankers or CEOs or rock stars. She knew she should feel grateful to have access to the *best path to the Ivies that money could buy*, as Daddy constantly reminded her. Daddy had taken out a second mortgage on the house in Brookline to pay for the tuition at St. Paul's so he could brag to his clients on the golf course.

But she didn't fit in. It wasn't just that she was fat—a fact that her mother never let her forget—it was that she really didn't like these people. Frankly she didn't think they liked each other very much— or even themselves for that matter.

What is it about rich kids? Candace thought. *They sleep through their morning classes, demand special accommodation for their phantom learning disabilities and fight with their teachers about their lousy grades. They threaten to bring the wrath of Daddy down onto the administration if their sexual assaults are prosecuted. You know what it is?* she decided, because she'd had a *lot* of time to think about it. *They are aware that they will never achieve a level of success to rival their parents; they are resigned to living off of trust funds and nepotism, pretending they're happy, pretending that they are the architects of their own lives.*

Okay, so maybe Daddy was right. Candace's dream was to attend Princeton—well, it was really Daddy's dream—but Candace wanted to please him, make him proud. She applied to Princeton for early decision and she had been checking her mailbox every day for a week. Then suddenly there it was—Ding!—like that—like the winning buzzer on *Jeopardy*—the letter from Princeton. She tore the envelope open, accidentally ripping the letter in half, and read it. Three times. She spread the pieces of the letter out on her desk, trying to smooth out the creases and then carefully taped it back together. She stuck the letter to her mirror and gazed into her reflection. *Princeton,* she thought. *Candace Parker is going to Princeton!* Instead of her round, doughy face, she imagined herself arriving on campus, skinny, her thighs no longer rubbing together, having lost twenty pounds over the summer.

She grabbed her phone and dialed Daddy's cell.

"Wonderful news!" he cried.

Next she texted Sara.

Awesome! Sara replied.

After posting the news on Facebook so that all of her Brookline friends would be jealous, she flopped onto her bed, grinning from ear-to-ear.

///

After Molly left, the dorm was eerily quiet except for the echo of a distant voice now and then, the slam of a door, the turn of a key in a lock. Candace wandered the halls, feeling melancholy. Outside a light snow was falling. She grabbed her down jacket and went out to enjoy the last few minutes of daylight. She stood in the quad looking up at the silent oaks and the gently falling snowflakes. Someone was walking along the path, toward her. As he approached, she recognized his unruly mane.

Danilo was an exchange student from Italy. He was definitely a "Paulie," but in a Euro-trash sort of way. His father was a banker with Credit Suisse in Milan. He had a mop of curly hair that he never combed and a wisp of a moustache.

He was in her Astronomy class.

"Scusi," she remembered him saying. It tickled her the way he pronounced Astronomy with the emphasis on the first syllable. "AST-ronomy!"

"Si," she said, thinking she sounded sophisticated.

They had not really spoken since, other than a smile, wave, or nod to acknowledge each other now and then.

"Danilo!" she called out.

"Ciao. You are leaving, no?"

"My plane isn't until nine," she said. "I don't know why I booked such a late flight. Everyone else is already gone. Are you staying here over the break?"

"I'm meeting my cousin in New York tomorrow," Danilo replied.

"I love Christmas in New York. It's my favorite time of year. The lights, the tree, the store windows," she said.

"The crowds, the honking horns, the puddles of slush on every corner," he said.

She laughed.

"Do you want to get a coffee?" he asked.

They walked in silence to Main Street and saw that The Old Europe was open. They settled into a booth and ordered—green tea for her, espresso for him.

"You'll stay with your cousin for the holidays?" she said.

"He has a loft in SoHo. It's cool. We might go skiing."

"Nice. And your parents? Will you see them?" she asked.

"My dad is in London and my mom is in China meeting with suppliers," he said. "They travel a lot. I don't see them much."

"Do you like it here, at St. Paul's?" Candace asked.

"It's okay. Not that different from my boarding school in London," Danilo said. "My dad wanted me to come here to *network with the Wall Street types*." Danilo punctuated the phrase with air quotes.

"And how is that going?" she asked with a smile. "The Paulies?"

"Oh my God! You call them that too?" She covered her face with her hands and convulsed in laughter.

"Everybody calls them that," he said. "They call themselves Paulies. It's ridiculous!"

"Really? Well, then who is not a Paulie?" she asked.

"I don't know. You? Me?" Danilo responded.

Candace started to question her value system. *So Danilo isn't a Paulie? Isn't he privileged and spoiled, a member of the one percent who will end up at*

Goldman Sachs and treat underlings—well everyone, really—with disdain?

"Do you really have to leave tonight?" he asked. "What if you stayed? Maybe we could see a movie? Catch a plane tomorrow? We could share a cab in the morning?"

Candace was taken aback. She had never been asked out by a boy. *Is this a date?* she wondered. *Maybe I can postpone my flight? I've never lied to my parents before, had never told them anything they wouldn't believe.* But now that she had been accepted into college—*into Princeton!*—she was filled with a new sense of confidence, that she could be in control of her life. *I can make my own decisions!*

"Let me make a call," she said.

She called the airline first.

She covered the phone and hissed at Danilo, "What time is your flight?"

"One p.m.."

"One p.m.?" she said into the phone. "One-ten? Perfect. Thank you. No, that's all. Thank you. Yes.

Thank you. Thank you. Okay. Thank you." She hung up.

"Okay, now Mommy. What should I say?" she asked.

"I don't know. You need extra time to pack?" he said.

"Oh, please!"

"Your roommate is throwing a party that you don't want to miss?" he suggested.

"Okay, that's better. She'll like that I'm bonding with the Paulies." They both convulsed in conspiratorial laughter.

"It's ringing," she hissed.

"Mommy? How are you, Mommy?" A pause. "Yes, I was good. Only low-carb today." Another pause. "I can't wait to see you, too. Um, I changed my flight—I'm coming in tomorrow afternoon, is that okay?" Another pause. "You know Molly, my roommate? Molly invited me to a holiday celebration tonight. Last minute. I'm sorry. Is that okay?" Pause. "I know, isn't that nice of her? Okay, Mommy, I'll

see you tomorrow. I'll text you my flight info."
Pause. "I love you, too." She hung up.

Candace's heart was racing. She had never lied to her mother before.

"Okay!" she said.

"Okay," he said.

"What now?"

"I don't know. Movie, dinner, my place?" he said.

"Yes!"

Two

N THE END, THEY ORDERED A PIZZA AND WENT TO HIS ROOM. They sat up for hours and talked. They talked about her family, his family. She told him about her upbringing in Brookline, a suburb of Boston. He told her about his childhood in Tuscany. Candace spoke with pride about her little sister, Sara, who was a star athlete in high school and was planning a career in sports medicine. Danilo spoke with disdain about his older brother, Lorenzo, who was a banker in London and was married to a French woman, Stephanie. He didn't think much of Stephanie. They had two bratty kids and a second home in the south of France.

"You're not eating your pizza," Danilo said.

Candace was mortified. *I was hoping you hadn't noticed,* she thought.

"I'm not hungry," she said. In fact, her stomach had been grumbling for hours, overwhelmed by the smell of sausage and pepperoni—but she was painfully aware that her muffin top was pressing against the waist of her jeans, threatening to burst the button.

"You're not one of those anorexic girls, are you?" he asked.

Anorexic? Does he think I look thin?

"Me?" she asked. "No!" She took a slice of pizza and gingerly picked at the toppings.

When she got tired, he covered her with a heavy quilt and cradled her head against his chest.

///

She woke up, not knowing where she was. The pillow smelled unfamiliar. *Why am I still in my jeans?*

She heard the flush of a toilet. Danilo walked in.

"Good morning," he said. He had showered and smelled fresh and spicy. *Like Old Spice,* she thought. He leaned down to kiss her and she recoiled. *My mouth tastes like road kill!*

"I'm sorry, I didn't mean to fall asleep. I have to go. I need to brush my teeth," she said.

"Oh, okay." He seemed hurt. "Do you want to get breakfast and then wait for the cab?"

The cab. Oh, right. Flustered, she clambered out of bed and dug around to find her shoes and her down jacket.

"Yes. Yes. Let me just get cleaned up and finish packing. I'll meet you in the Great Hall and we'll grab brunch. What time is the cab?" She was clearly disoriented. "Oh geez, what time is it?"

"It's eight-thirty," he said. "The cab isn't coming until eleven-thirty. You have plenty of time. Can I walk you back to your dorm?"

"No, no. I'm good," she said. "Give me an hour. I'll meet you in the Great Hall, okay?"

Candace was surprised to find herself smiling as she walked back to her dorm in the brisk morning air. She wasn't sure how she felt about Danilo, wasn't really sure if she could trust him. She had not dated at St. Paul's, or at all, really. She was wary of the Paulies, afraid of what they really thought of her—a fat, bourgeois chick, she assumed. She feared being taken advantage of and becoming the victim of a social media shaming—reduced to a stream of naked photos that circulated around campus. She had seen first-hand how badly that ended. One afternoon she walked into her dorm room to find Molly and Molly's friend, Perry, giggling over their smart phones.

"What a slut!" Molly exclaimed.

"Who?" Candace asked.

"Oh, I didn't see you there." Molly and Perry hurriedly closed their Instagram apps.

Candace didn't need to ask. She had a pretty good idea of what they were looking at. *Thank God that's not me!* she had thought.

But last night was so nice. Up talking all night, cuddling, falling asleep on his shoulder. What if? she thought. *What if we became a couple?* She felt all warm inside. *What if I had someone to hold hands with and stroll around campus? Someone to meet in the library and go out for hot chocolate or ice cream? Someone to take me to prom?*

She showered and finished packing in a rush and ran down to the Great Hall with wet hair, hoping she wasn't late. The hall was deserted. He wasn't there. A wave of emotions rolled over her: humiliation, anger, self-recrimination. *Now I have to go to the airport with wet hair. What an idiot!*

She opened the door to look outside. Nothing. She turned back toward the stairwell and her roller bag got stuck in the door.

"Bella mia!" Dilano shouted from across the quad.

She froze in place and turned toward his voice. *Why do Paulies have such large luggage?* she wondered as she watched him trudging toward her, dragging his oversized suitcase across the frozen lawn.

He reached her and put a hand behind her head and pulled her face in for a kiss. She stiffened at first but then melted into him. *Man, he is a good kisser!*

"Ah, minty fresh," he said. He still held her head in his palm and their eyes were inches apart. She noticed how complex his were, irises that were rings of green and brown flecked with gold.

"My hair is wet," she said.

"Yes. Do you want to dry it?" he said. "We have time. Your hair will freeze in the cold air."

"I'll use the ladies room. I'll just be a minute," she said.

"I'll be here," he said.

In the bathroom, she stared into the mirror. "Get a grip," she said to the mirror. "Pull yourself together." She dug her hairdryer and makeup bag out of her suitcase. A few minutes later she surveyed the results and deemed them quite good.

"You look great," he said when she rejoined him. "Now, breakfast?"

They dragged their bags across the quad and down to Main Street, where they found a booth at The Old Europe and ordered tapas to share.

Candace watched with envy as Danilo wolfed his food.

"Eat, Bella," he said with his mouth full.

Candace smiled demurely and took tiny bites.

Eat slow, her mother always said. *Give your brain time to signal that your stomach is full. This actually works!* Candace thought. After a couple of bites, she already felt full. *What if we were a couple? What if having a boyfriend meant never feeling hungry again? What if I were a skinny girl?*

"You're smiling," Danilo said. "What's funny?"

"Nothing is funny," Candace said. "I'm just happy today, in this moment, here with you."

Danilo looked at her with a quizzical smile on his face.

Oh, God, what have I said! What is he thinking?

"Yes," he said at last. "This is nice."

//

The cab arrived at the appointed time and took them to the Manchester airport.

Candace waited in line with Danilo as he checked his enormous bag.

"What have you got in there?" she asked, laughing.

Danilo bristled. "You don't need to wait with me."

Candace blushed. "No, it's okay."

Mercifully, the line was short and a few minutes later they were through security and on the concourse.

Danilo turned to Candace and said, "Ciao for now. See you in January."

"Text me?" she said.

"Sure," he replied.

///

Candace dragged her bag to her gate and found a seat. She pulled out her iPhone. There was a text from her mother, What time is your flight?

Oh, shit! I forgot to text her.

I'm on the 1:10, Candace texted.

You're just telling me now? Candace could hear the fury behind her mother's typing.

I'm sorry, Candace texted. I overslept. I just got to the airport.

A few minutes went by. Candace imagined her mother screaming at Daddy for several minutes about what a fuck-up Candace was and then Daddy searching for the flight info to see what time it arrived in Logan.

Sure enough, her father texted: Meet me on the upper level.

Three

NORMALLY, CHRISTMAS WAS CANDACE'S FAVORITE TIME of year. It was the one time of the year that Mommy and Daddy could be relied upon to get along without quarreling—when the Parker family seemed happy. Every year, Daddy would take them to Beverly Tree Farm to find the perfect tree. And then they'd all climb into the attic to bring down the boxes of decorations. Then there was the ritual of sorting through ornaments from generations of Parkers and Swifts, Mommy gently cradling each one and sharing the history again, year after year, before gingerly handing them over to Candace and Sara to hang them, just so. Then there was the issue of tinsel. Sara tossed the tinsel all over the place, so that it landed in huge clumps that clung to the larger branches. At that point Mommy would swoop in to separate the clumps into individual strands and Candace would step out of the fray, relaxing on the couch with a bowl of Hershey's kisses and watch Mommy make everything perfect.

This year was different. Candace was distracted; she couldn't put her iPhone down, anxiously hoping and praying for a text. *What is Danilo doing right now?*

The doorbell rang. Sara answered it and returned to the living room with a slender FedEx box.

"What's that? Mommy asked.

"It's for Candace," Sara said.

"Let me see," Candace said. She jumped up and grabbed the box out of Sara's hands, tearing it open to find an elegantly wrapped package. She read the card. "Thinking of you. Danilo."

Oh my God, Danilo sent me a gift. Her heart raced. *He likes me!* Then horror set it. *I didn't send him anything!*

"What is it, Candace?" Mommy said.

"It's from a boy at school," Candace said.

"A boy?" Sara said. "You haven't said anything about a boy! Must tell!"

"Oh, Mommy!" Candace cried. "I didn't get him anything. What should I do?"

"Well, who is this boy?" Mommy said.

"Danilo. He's an Italian exchange student. We met in September but only recently became friends—last week, actually. I can't believe he sent me a gift. That's so unfair! What do I do now?"

"Well, you say thank you. You're not obligated to give him a gift. You've only just become friends," Mommy said.

Mothers give such terrible advice.

Sara had a better idea. "Let's open it and then FedEx him something back."

Candace texted, Ur package arrived :)

He replied, Merry Xmas :)

Candace gently removed the tape and peeled back the wrapping paper.

It was a vinyl LP—the soundtrack to *Garden State.*

"Oh shit! What do we do now?" Candace said.

Sara was full of suggestions. "*Cerulean Salt* by Waxahatchee or *Are We There* by Sharon Von Etten or *James Blake* by James Blake or *Inni* by Sigur Ros or *For Emma, Forever Ago* by Bon Iver."

"Seriously?" Candace said. "You rock! Which one, which one?"

"Um, I'm thinking Bon Iver. He'll think you're a real hipster, not some chubby dork who's never seen an indie band," Sara said.

"Gee, thanks," Candace said, punching Sara in the arm.

The girls ran upstairs to Sara's room and ordered the album off of vinylloop.com.

"Vinyl Loop? How do you know about these things, little sister?" Candace punched Sara in the arm again.

"Ouch!" Sara said. "You're so out of it, all isolated up there in your snooty boarding school."

The girls huddled together over the keyboard to place the order, gift-wrapped with overnight delivery to the address on the FedEx package.

"What if this isn't where his cousin lives?" Candace asked.

Sara MapQuested 53 Howard Street. "Yup, that's in SoHo. This has to be the right place."

Sara hit PLACE ORDER and they both let out a squeal of delight.

"Now we wait," Candace said.

///

The next morning at breakfast, Candace was glued to her phone.

"What time does FedEx deliver?" she asked.

"Well, that depends," Mommy said. "Did you order morning or afternoon delivery?"

"Shit!" Candace hissed at Sara. "Did we order morning or afternoon?"

"We ordered Priority—what is that, morning or afternoon?" Sara said.

"It should arrive by ten thirty." Mommy looked up at the clock. "Any minute."

Ping, Candace's phone displayed a message alert.

Ur package arrived. I put it under the tree, Danilo texted.

Me too, Candace lied.

What are you doing today? she texted.

Ice skating in Bryant Park. Maybe a movie later, he replied. And you?

Mani-pedi with Sis and old friends from middle school. Maybe a movie later.

Have fun, Danilo texted.

You too. Ciao, she replied.

//

But Candace couldn't have fun. Danilo's life seemed so much more exciting than hers. She wished she were spending Christmas in New York with his rich relatives, shopping for luxury goods in SoHo and dining out every night. She imagined walking through Central Park as snow fell in the fading light of the day. *Maybe there is a dog in the picture. Yes, certainly a dog! A Dalmatian—or a Great Dane—we have a big dog because we live in a big loft in SoHo. And on Christmas Eve we'll meet all of our rich relatives at Balthazar's for a huge feast and the walls will be all twinkly with little white lights and people on the street will gaze through the windows with envy.*

"My life sucks," Candace groused. She and Sara sat side by side, drying their nails at the salon.

"If your life sucks, that means my life sucks too," Sara replied. "And my life definitely doesn't suck. You know my volleyball team is going to nationals, right?"

"No," Candace said. "Your life is blessed. Look at you, all tall and athletic. You're the captain of every fucking sports team at Brookline High. And look at me—all short and marshmallow-y. I'm captain of nothing."

"At least you're going to Princeton," Sara said. "That's not nothing. Daddy is thrilled!"

"Of course he's thrilled," Candace said darkly. "That's his dream, not mine."

"What is your dream?" Sara asked.

Candace thought about that. Nobody had ever asked her that before. Ever since she was ten years old, Daddy had been talking about Princeton. Even before Candace knew what the Ivy League was she knew that Princeton was the best college in the universe. And she was going to go there, if Daddy had any say in the matter.

"I don't know," Candace said. "Go to a college where I'm not the fattest, poorest girl on campus? Do you know what it's like being surrounded by ridiculously rich, skinny bitches?"

"There are plenty of rich, skinny bitches at Brookline High," Sara said.

"Well, at least you got the skinny part right," Candace said.

//

When Christmas morning arrived, Candace got another text.

Bon Iver? Danilo texted. Wow! Love it! How did you know I'm into vinyl?

Because—duh—you sent ME vinyl. But then she realized that she supposedly hadn't opened the package until just now.

Candace yelled to Sara, "What do I say, what do I say?"

Sara grabbed the phone and texted back, I guess we have more in common than we knew.

And then a second text, I LOVE Garden State! Can't wait to see you in January.

He replied with a smiley face.

Candace grabbed the phone back. "What? I can't wait to see you! What have you done?"

Sara collapsed in a fit of giggles and Candace pummeled her with a throw pillow.

Four

CANDACE WAS NERVOUS AND ELATED TO RETURN TO campus. Daddy drove her back to school in his battered Subaru.

"Thanks, Daddy!" Candace grabbed her bag and slammed the hatchback.

"Wait! Two hours in traffic to get up here? I thought we'd grab lunch or something?" Daddy said.

"Sorry, Daddy. Molly texted me—she said there is a party to go to. I need to unpack and get changed." She threw him a kiss. "Thanks for the ride. Love you!" Candace felt Daddy's eyes observing her in the rearview mirror as he pulled out. Candace did not look back.

Candace entered her room to find Molly sprawled on the bed.

"How was your Christmas?" Candace asked.

"Hellish! My luggage got lost. I had to sit in the condo for days while everyone was out skiing. Then a huge storm blew through and we lost power. Fucking freezing!" Molly said.

"I'm so sorry. Mine was nice, thanks for asking," Candace said. "Danilo sent me a vinyl album."

"Who? The Italian guy? No shit! He gave you a gift? You two are an item?" Molly asked. "When did this happen?"

"I know!" Candace said. "I'm so nervous about seeing him this week. What do you think? Are we a couple?"

"Shit, yeah! If he gave you a Christmas present," Molly said. "That's a commitment. What did you give him?"

"I FedExed him a Bon Iver vinyl," Candace said.

"Bon Iver? Really? I underestimated you, my roomie," Molly said.

"It was my little sister Sara's idea," Candace said. "At fifteen she is cooler than me, really."

"You set the bar pretty low, my roomie, pretty darn low," Molly said. "Kids today! You want to go down to the dining hall and see who's back?"

What a bitch, she thought. *Can't she say one nice thing to me?* But she dutifully followed Molly downstairs.

Ping, Candace's phone displayed a message alert.

R U back? It was Danilo.

Ya, she replied.

Meet me in the dining hall?

Heading down now, she texted.

Molly and Candace rounded the corner and there he was. Molly peeled away.

"Hi Danilo. See you later, C," Molly said.

"Hi," he said.

"Hi," she said. *Okay, this is like the dumbest conversation ever! What would Sara say?*

"Bon Iver, huh?" he asked.

"I hope you really liked it and weren't just saying

that." *Well, how is he supposed to answer that?* she wondered. *Geez!*

He laughed and she relaxed. They walked together into the dining hall and entered the queue.

While they ate, Danilo made small talk, chatting about his holiday in New York. What they had done, where they had gone, what designer products they had purchased. Candace sat silently smiling and nodding. She didn't say much, but then again he hadn't asked her a single question about her holiday. And then when he was done with his meal, Danilo said, "Ciao," and walked away. Just like that. Candace didn't know what to think. First he sends a Christmas gift and then he texts: *can't wait to see you. Oh wait, that was me! Dammit Sara!*

But then it happened again the next day. Danilo materialized by her side in the lunch line and sat with her. And again, he talked about his day, his classes, his demanding parents. Candace wasn't sure exactly how it happened but she started taking it for granted that they would eat lunch together every day. And study together in the library. Then it turned into a standing date every Friday. On Friday at lunch they checked out the listings for campus performances—music, comedy, dance, theater, maybe a movie—they would pick something and go together. And at the end of the evening, Danilo walked Candace back to her dorm.

Candace felt beautiful every time Danilo looked at her. That had never happened to her before. She was becoming someone she had always envied. Someone with a boyfriend. She had never had a boyfriend before. There were so many things she didn't understand. *What was the protocol? Who would make the first move?* Her friends back home hadn't dated any more than she had. There was no one that she could talk to about Danilo.

//

But then this one time, as they walked together along the sidewalk, he stopped abruptly and spun Candace toward the plate glass window of the building entrance. He grabbed her hands from behind and swung them up above her head and then down. Up and down, like a standing jumping jack. She giggled and squealed, "What are you doing?" And then she caught sight of her reflection in the glass, her muffin top belly peeking out from under her tee shirt with each swing. Her face reddened and she jerked her arms away from him. "Stop it!" *Is he making fun of me?* she wondered. *Is this an innocent flirtation, or something more sinister?*

She wanted to get away from him; she thought about running back to her dorm, but that would be so awkward. So she walked with him in silence and when they reached the lobby, he took her hand as he always did, swung it childishly to and fro and said goodnight. Like always, like nothing had happened. *Maybe nothing had.* Candace was confused.

It became more and more awkward, the nightly parting in the lobby of her dorm. At first it involved interlaced fingers, then a clumsy hug, then a chaste peck and finally a goodnight kiss that became the norm. But she could never shake the nagging memory of the weird jumping-jack episode.

Of course, eventually the kisses became longer, wetter and gradually involved tongue. This was all new to Candace; the physical desire mixed with fear created a heightened sense of excitement. Her parents had never talked to her about going too far with a boy. She was the daughter they never worried about. She was the sensible one. There was no reason to waste their time talking to the daughter who didn't date.

"Do you want to come up to my room?" Danilo finally asked.

Candace had been waiting for this moment since the day before Christmas break. *He likes me!* She immediately thought that she should run back to her room and take a shower. *What if my pits stink?*

"Um, sure," she said.

The first time Danilo tried to unbutton her blouse she wouldn't let him. She pushed his hand away and kissed him. The trouble was, she didn't want to stop him. Everywhere he touched her felt wonderful, like some sort soft, hot glow. But eventually she pulled herself away and made some excuse to leave.

After a few weeks she didn't stop him, anymore. She didn't care. When he stroked her breasts and when he slid his finger inside her panties, she didn't want him to quit, she wanted them to stay where they were forever. It felt wonderful. She'd never realized how wonderful it would feel.

///

Candace and Danilo trudged through the snow blanketing the Meadow on their way to math class in Lindsay Hall.

"I hate snow," Danilo said.

"Really?" Candace said. "This is kind of awkward, then. I should have asked earlier, but my parents wanted to know if you would like to go skiing with us in Vermont over spring break?" She'd been practicing this for weeks and hoped she sounded casual and nonchalant.

"I don't mind the snow in the mountains. I just don't want to have to deal with it every day," Danilo said.

They walked together for a few minutes and Danilo still hadn't answered the question. "So. . . what do you think?" Candace asked. She hoped she didn't sound desperate.

"That's very kind of your parents," Danilo said. "My cousin is expecting me in New York but I'm sure he'd rather I find somewhere else to go."

"So, you'll come?" she said.

"Sure, why not?" he said.

Candace didn't know what to think. *Sure, why not? He doesn't sound very excited.*

Five

CANDACE WAS MORTIFIED WHEN DADDY INFORMED HER THAT they would be driving to Vermont.

"In the Subaru?" she cried.

"Is there something wrong with the Subaru? I took out a second mortgage to send you to that hoity-toity school and now you're too good for us? This is the thanks I get?"

"I'm sorry, Daddy," Candace said. "But, how are we all going to fit? Three of us in the back seat for five hours? What if we just met you up there?"

"Who is going to pay for that? This condo is costing me an arm and a leg. Your mother insisted on a skiing vacation this year. Good God, with the lift tickets and the condo rental, do you know what this is costing me? Now I'm supposed to rent a minivan?"

"Could you, Daddy? With the skis and the bags and five of us and all, don't you think we'll need a bigger car?"

"Oh my God, you're just like your mother! George, buy me this, we need that, can't we have something bigger?"

Candace had already tuned him out.

"Fine!" he shouted.

The line went dead. He had hung up her. Candace had won. *Now what to wear?*

Danilo seems to like me just the way I am. Pleasingly plump, voluptuous, curvy? Maybe that is his thing? But she knew she looked like an over-stuffed sausage in her spandex ski bib. She opted for jeans, turtleneck sweaters in a rainbow of pastel colors and an oversized pastel down jacket.

On Saturday morning, Candace stood in the parking lot with her suitcase, nervously waiting for Danilo to arrive. He appeared with his oversized luggage and his Rosignol skis in a custom case. Silently she thanked her father for springing for the minivan. Danilo's baggage would have never fit into the Subaru.

"Bella mia." Danilo leaned in and gave her a wet kiss. Her heart raced.

"This should be a fun trip," she said. "But, I've warned you about my parents. I'm not sure they really like me."

"Candace, please, parents suck," he said. "Mine text me from London or Shanghai or Milan. They are so busy with their lives, I don't even know why they ever bothered to have children. They don't speak to each other, and they haven't spoken to me in months. I am nothing to them."

Candace felt really sad for him. Her parents were cold and demanding but it would be much worse if they just ignored her.

Daddy pulled up in a Cadillac Escalade and Candace immediately regretted asking him to rent a car. Both her parents were decked out in brand new parkas. *What have I done? I'll be hearing about this for months.* "Do you know what that cost me? Plus the upgrade to the deluxe condo? I hope this boy is worth it!"

If Danilo was uncomfortable, he didn't show it. He exchanged idle chatter with Candace's parents and Sara all the way to Sugar Bush, acting as if he had known them forever. Candace was in awe. *How do the Paulies do it?* she wondered. *Are they born with refined social skills?*

Darkness fell as they pulled into the town of Warren.

"Anybody hungry?" Daddy asked.

There was a chorus of "me" in reply.

Daddy pulled into the parking lot of The Common Man.

"This place is supposed to be good," he said.

The restaurant was massive—room after room, each with a fireplace and stone walls. They were guided to a table next to a family of seven with two small children who were talking loudly and banging their spoons on the table.

"Who brings toddlers to a ski resort?" hissed Mommy.

"They probably ski better than me," said Candace.

"Everybody skis better than you," said Sara.

Candace looked at Danilo and grimaced. His demeanor was placid.

Daddy did most of the talking at dinner, asking Danilo about his major, his family, his plans for the future. Candace was mostly mute, admiring his unruffled performance.

As they arrived at the condo, Daddy made a big display of the spaciousness and opulence and pointed out that there were three bedrooms—one for Danilo in the adjacent wing. Danilo and Candace exchanged wistful glances as they headed for their rooms.

"This whole thing is a mistake," Candace said as she climbed into bed.

"You should have booked your own condo," Sara said.

"Don't be ridiculous," Candace said. "I just mean that it's too soon to be meeting the 'rents. We're not even serious. Why did I invite him? Why did he even agree to come?"

"You're not serious? Mommy said this might be your last chance."

"What am I, thirty?" Candace exclaimed. *Jesus, I*

just got accepted to Princeton. Why can't that be enough for them?

"Hey, you invited him. It's your funeral," Sara said.

Candace bit into the dinner roll she had pirated from the restaurant. *My jeans are not going to fit me tomorrow,* she thought.

//

Candace awoke to the smell of bacon and coffee. Mommy was dishing up waffles to Danilo.

"Good morning," Candace said to nobody in particular.

"Bella mia!"

Sure, Candace thought, *you're charming in the morning, too.*

Mommy was all decked out in her designer skiwear. Candace was still in her baggy flannel pajamas.

"Candace." Mommy's voice took on an edge. "We'll want to be on the lift at nine. Will you be ready?"

All Candace wanted to do was inhale a waffle and fall back into bed.

"Sure, Mommy," she said.

As she left the room, she heard Mommy saying to Danilo, "I don't know what you see in her."

//

Candace took a break from skiing at lunch while Danilo joined Daddy for several more runs. She saw Mommy and Sara at a table on the deck and clomped over in her ski boots to join them.

Mommy surveyed Candace's tray. "French fries?" she said.

"I'm hungry. I didn't have breakfast," Candace said.

"You should always eat breakfast," Mommy said. Then turning to Sara, she said, "Didn't you want to make another run with Daddy?"

Sara got the hint, gathered up her tray, and headed outside.

"Danilo seems nice," Mommy said.

"Yes."

"You probably shouldn't get too serious. He's going back to Europe for college and you're going to Princeton."

"I knew this was a mistake," Candace said. "We're not serious. We're just friends. I like him. But I shouldn't have invited him. I don't know what I was thinking."

"Well he's very nice, very well-bred," Mommy said. "We're happy to have made his acquaintance."

Candace wondered if Mommy was regretting the outlay on the condo, the Escalade, the fancy new ski togs.

//

Candace suffered through three more days of forced merriment, frozen mittens, and soggy fries from the snack bar. Falling into bed, exhausted by eight. Wakened by the smell of a hearty breakfast that Candace wasn't allowed to eat. Finally the week ended and they were headed home.

Back at St. Paul's, Daddy got out to help Danilo with the luggage.

"Well, Danilo, it was very nice to meet you." They shook hands. "I hope you had a good time. Candace, baby, love you," he said as he crushed her in his massive bear hug. "See you in May? Study hard. Keep up the good work."

And then they were gone. Candace and Danilo stood with their luggage and skis in the entryway to the Grand Hall.

"Um, sorry about all of that," Candace said. "Did you have fun?"

"I enjoy you and your family," he said. "Sara is very fun."

"Yes," she said, relieved. She leaned against him and he put his arm around her. She felt so much better, alone with him again, away from her parents.

Six

OR BETTER OR WORSE, THE SKI TRIP HAD BROUGHT THEM closer together. He seemed less formal, she felt more relaxed around him. One Friday night, as he was walking her home after a movie, they lingered in the Meadow, kissing.

"I don't want to go home," she said.

"No?"

"Can I stay with you tonight? All night?" she asked.

"Sure. All night? What about curfew?" Danilo asked.

"I'll text Molly. She'll be cool."

"Okay," he said.

"I want to be with you," she said. "I'm ready."

"You're ready? For the sex? Oh." He hesitated. "No, that's great. Um, I should pick up some condoms. Can we make it to the pharmacy before they close?"

"You don't have condoms?" she asked.

"I know, stupid, right?" He started fumbling in his pocket for his phone. "What time do they close?"

Candace was tired. She didn't feel like walking all the way to Main Street. Once, in middle school, she saw a rubber on the ground and everyone walked around it and laughed. Candace couldn't imagine using something like that. *And besides, wouldn't that spoil the mood? Standing in line at CVS in the glare of florescent lighting?*

///

"It's okay. I have protection," she lied. "And I don't have AIDS or herpes or anything—do you?" Candace's knowledge was limited. Apparently her mother hadn't worried that the sex question would ever come up. *What boy would want to have sex with such a hideous creature?* Candace had heard there were things you could use after having unprotected sex—like douches. *They work, right? Or wasn't there a morning-after pill?*

"No, no. Of course not the AIDS," he said.

"Or herpes?"

"No, of course not," he said.

"Okay, then." She was feeling bold and empowered, in control of her sexuality. This would be her first time, but he didn't need to know that.

He seemed more nervous than she as he fumbled with the lock on his door. But his confidence returned as they groped each other in the darkness. He deftly removed her bra and lowered her gently to the bed, sliding her panties over her thighs and past her toes.

She was grateful for the dark.

"You feel great!" he said. *As opposed to how I look?* she thought. *To his hands, I imagine I feel beautiful. Handfuls of warm flesh.* He cupped her breasts and she was suddenly self-conscious about their heft and looseness, and she was afraid that he would be grossed out. But no, he seemed turned on.

"You sure this is okay?" he said breathlessly as he pressed himself against her.

She was startled at how hard his penis was. It hurt as he pressed it against her thigh and then her belly.

"Yes, I'm sure," she said.

Of course she wasn't sure. She had no idea what was coming next. And, ow! It hurt. *Is it supposed to hurt like this?*

He was moaning. So she started moaning in rhythm with him. "Yes, yes, yes." Thinking, *ow, ow, ow.*

"Can I come?" he said. "In Italy, we come in the anus. You want me to come in the anus?

"No," she said. *Gross!* she thought.

Soon enough it was over. He grunted and then let out a little giggle.

"Oh, that was good," he said as he rolled onto his back.

She was thinking, *What am I supposed to say? I'm glad? You're welcome? Thank you?*

But, he was already snoring.

In the morning, he wanted to go again. She wasn't wet so he went down on her. She was afraid that she smelled bad, her breath, her B.O. But he didn't seem to care. She was surprised by the warmth and deliciousness that flooded through her and overwhelmed her until she was shaking. This time when he entered her, she was ready and she pressed her mouth to his, forgetting her self-consciousness, and lost herself in him. When he was done, she was still floating on a wave of abandon and ecstasy.

She wondered, *Was that an orgasm? So this is sex? I think I like this.* She chuckled.

"What's funny?" he mumbled, half-asleep.

"That was fun," she said.

"Yes," he said and he held her tighter.

//

After that he wanted it every day.

Candace realized that she needed to go to the clinic and get the pill or a diaphragm or an IUD. Molly and the others talked about it all the time. Orgasms, oral sex, anal sex, abortions, STDs, and protection. She called the clinic and made an appointment, but the waiting list was two weeks long. And yet, because she had told him it was safe, she didn't object or resist his advances even as she counted the days down to the appointment at the clinic.

Everything was different once they started having sex. All of a sudden the long hours they'd spent in the library and seeing movies were gone. The time they spent together seemed much more rushed and frantic. And when they had sex it would all be over in just a few minutes. It was all so hurried and almost rough, and it made her think that having sex had taken her to a completely different world.

Most of the time Danilo only acted tender and loving after he'd come. That the only time he seemed to notice her. Sometimes when he was thrusting and pushing in her, she felt like it could have been anyone. It didn't matter who she was or whether she was enjoying it. He never noticed, one way or another. But, she just wanted to make him happy.

Candace realized how easy it was to have sex but how hard it was to talk about it. They never talked about it. After they had started having sex, they never talked much about anything. They never looked each other in the face. The more they had sex the further apart they seemed.

Candace usually felt like crying when it was over. She wasn't sure why. She just felt sad. He'd finish and she'd have tears rolling down her cheeks. At those times Danilo would hold her but it never made her feel much better.

//

Candace sat in the waiting room of the clinic with dozens of other students, victims of athletic mishaps, colds, flu, allergies, and an incident involving a swarm of bees. Candace sat in bemused silence and eavesdropped on the patients and nursing staff.

"Candace Parker!"

She jumped as her name was called and clumsily gathered her purse and sweater.

"Follow me, dear," the nurse said.

Candace followed her into the exam room. The nurse shut the door.

"You're here for a pelvic exam?" The nurse made some notes on a clipboard.

"Yes," Candace replied. "Birth control."

The nurse looks up. "Are you sexually active?"

"Yes, I have a boyfriend," Candace said.

"Are you using protection?" the nurse said.

"Yes," Candace lied, feeling her face getting hot.

"Did you leave a urine sample at the nurses' station?" the nurse said.

"I tried but I couldn't go," Candace said.

"Try again when the doctor is done with the exam. Make sure you leave a sample before you go. Now take off your shoes and step on the scale, please."

Candace sucked in her breath and closed her eyes

as she heard the nurse nudge the sliding weight to the right, all the way to the right. Then she moved the counter weight up a notch and nudged the sliding weight over again until the horizontal beam finally balanced.

"One sixty-three," the nurse said. "Now your height." She raised the height rod and pressed it on the crown of Candace's head. "Five feet and four and a half inches."

Candace was mortified. *One-sixty-three? That can't be!* She started sweating and her heart began to race. Through a fog she saw the nurse's lips moving, but she wasn't comprehending.

"I'm sorry?" Candace said.

"Have a seat and roll up your sleeve so I can check your blood pressure."

The nurse wrapped the Velcro cuff around Candace's arm. The machine made a whirring noise and the cuff squeezed tight around Candace's bicep.

"Ow!"

"Now don't be a baby," the nurse said, scowling.

These spoiled rich kids, Candace was sure she was thinking.

"One-forty over ninety."

"Is that good?" said Candace.

"It's a little on the high side. You should watch your salt intake," the nurse said, making more notes on the clipboard. She then spun on her heel and left the room.

Seven

Slowly, Candace stepped out of her jeans and panties and then tugged her tee shirt over her head. Standing in her bra, she glimpsed herself in the mirror. *What a pig,* she thought. *I never want Danilo to see me naked. Gross!*

She waited on the table for what seemed like forever, feeling exposed in the flimsy paper gown and sheet that kept slipping off of her.

A knock on the door, and the doctor entered.

"I'm Dr. Rosenberg," she said as she extended her hand.

Candace reached to shake the doctor's hand and the sheet began to slip again. She clutched at the sheet and the doctor smiled warmly.

"A little nervous today? Is this your first pelvic exam?" asked Dr. Rosenberg.

"I guess." said Candace. "Will this hurt?"

"Some girls find it a little uncomfortable. We'll see how you do." Dr. Rosenberg sat on a low stool and picked up a clipboard. "Let's see. Are you having any symptoms?"

"Symptoms?" Candace said.

"In general—fever, headache, cramps, discharge? How are you feeling, in general?"

"Fine."

"How old were you when you got your first period?"

"Um." Candace had to think. "Eleven? Twelve?"

"And when did your breasts develop?"

Candace blushed at the thought, remembering fifth grade. "Fifth grade?"

"Getting younger and younger," Dr. Rosenberg said to herself. "Are you getting regular periods? Every four weeks?"

"I don't really know," Candace said. "Sometimes four and sometimes more."

"That's perfectly normal." Dr. Rosenberg's pen scratched on the clipboard. "When was your last period?"

Candace thought hard. *The ski trip? Right, I got my period on the last day of the trip. I had forgotten to pack tampons and Mommy had to make an emergency run to the Walgreens.* Now it all came back to her.

"February break," Candace said.

"How heavy would you say they are? How many tampons do you use in a day?"

Candace wondered what all this information was leading to. *Was Dr. Rosenberg going to have an epiphany?*

"I don't know," she answered.

"You're sexually active?"

"Yes," Candace said.

"How many partners do you have?" asked Dr. Rosenberg.

"I have a boyfriend. He's the only one," Candace said. *Is Danilo my boyfriend?*

"And you're sure he's monogamous?"

Monogamous? Candace's face got hot.

"How would I know that?" she said.

"He's one of those, huh?" Dr. Rosenberg pushed her glasses up on her nose and gave Candace a stern look. "Why do you put up with that? On-again, off-again. Comes around for a booty call. Don't waste your time, my dear!"

Candace laughed. *This kind of frank talk isn't what I expected to hear from a gynecologist.*

"Here's what we're going to do. This is a speculum." She held up a silver instrument that reminded Candace of something her mother might use for potting plants. "I've warmed it to body temperature and I'm going to insert this into your vagina. You'll feel some pressure as I open it to see your vaginal canal and your cervix. Would you like a mirror so you can see?"

"No, thank you," Candace said. *Gross!*

Dr. Rosenberg continued. "I'm going to look at your cervix and take a tissue sample for the lab. It's like a giant Q-tip that we might use to take a sample from the inside of your cheek. I'll press on your abdomen to check the size and shape of your uterus and ovaries. Just to make sure everything is okay. Ready?"

Candace nodded solemnly.

"Okay, put your feet in the stirrups and lie back. Now slide your bottom toward the end of the table. A little farther, farther. Okay, right there. Now breathe slowly and relax. Let your knees fall to each side allowing your legs to spread apart. This will only take a minute or two."

"Yikes!" Candace yelped as the doctor started the exam.

"Honey, I'm going to need you to stay still. Try humming to distract yourself. We're almost done," the doctor said.

And then a clank of metal and Candace felt the speculum slide out. *Relief!*

The doctor stood over her and untied the robe. "Let me just check your breasts. Pay attention to what I'm doing. You should perform self-exams every month. First the right"—she palpated Candace's breast—"and the left. Okay, good girl. We're done. Sit up and cover up."

The doctor sat on a low stool next to Candace. "What type of birth control were you thinking of? We have many alternatives: pills, patches, diaphragm, IUD, cervical cap . . . "

"What's the easiest?" Candace said. "I mean the one I'm least likely to screw up?"

"I'd recommend an Ortho Evra patch. Most girls find it easy to use. You put on a new patch once a week for three weeks in a row. A lot of girls wear them on their hipbone or on their lower back. In the fourth week, you don't wear a patch and that week you should have a period. You always change your patch on the same day. Sound good?"

Candace nodded and Dr. Rosenberg wrote the prescription.

"Now be sure to use this along with condoms," she said, handing Candace the slip of paper. "This patch won't protect you from STDs like chlamydia, gonorrhea or herpes. I want you to schedule a follow-up appointment for next month so we can see how well you're tolerating the medication."

As Candace got dressed she thought about what

Dr. Rosenberg had said about STDs. *Herpes would be the worst!* She marched out of the clinic determined to talk to Danilo about using a condom and completely forgot about leaving a urine sample.

//

That evening in the dining hall, Danilo and Candace sat down where Molly and a group of her friends were talking about spring break.

"Hey, Candy, what do you think about the Bahamas?" Molly said. "My brother's team is competing in a regatta and they need volunteers."

"Volunteers to do what?" asked Danilo.

"Oh you know, help with the boats, flags, judging, all kinds of stuff," said Molly.

"Where would we stay?" asked Candace.

"The team is being hosted by local families," Molly said. "We'll be assigned to a family; they even feed us. All we need to pay for is airfare and our bar tab."

Danilo grinned broadly. "We're in!"

"You are?" Candace said. "I mean, we are?"

"Don't worry, kid." Danilo said. "If you need some help with the airfare, I can lend you some money."

"Oh. Okay. I guess it sounds like fun," Candace said, wondering if she should tell her parents or make up another story. She was still worrying over it when Danilo dropped her back at her dorm. But then her concern turned to what she was going to wear.

In the end, she told her parents that Danilo had invited her to the Bahamas and left it at that. Mommy even offered to take her shopping for beach clothes, so Candace booked a train to Boston for the following weekend.

///

Mommy met Candace at South Station and did not even try to hide her disgust.

"Candace! You look like a stuffed sausage!" Mommy gasped.

"Geez, Mommy," Candace said, tears in her eyes.

"You must have put on ten pounds, just since Christmas," Mommy went on.

"Mommy, people are looking."

"Who is looking?" Mommy asked. Then she turned to a couple of middle-aged women who were standing nearby and said, "Mind your own business!"

"Mommy, not them. Other people. Please, can we talk about this at home?"

"What about Lord and Taylor?" Mommy said. "I want to go to Lord and Taylor and check out the sale."

"I'm tired now, Mommy," Candace said. "Can we go tomorrow?"

"We'll have to shop in the plus-size section," Mommy muttered. "Alright, tomorrow. Nothing but cottage cheese and fruit for you tonight, young lady."

///

After a day of humiliation in the mirrored changing

rooms at Lord and Taylor, Candace was even more self-conscious about her body. She decided to pack only gym shorts and baggy tee shirts for the trip. *I'll explain to everyone that I forgot to pack my bathing suit.*

Eight

WHEN THEY LANDED IN THE BAHAMAS, CANDACE, MOLLY and the others took a taxi to the yacht club where the party was well under way. Men of all ages were congregated in the open-air bar and around the pool, drinking Bahama Mamas and rum punch.

"Where are the girls?" Candace asked.

"We *are* the girls," Molly replied.

Molly spotted her brother, Nick, at the bar and waved. "I'm going to go get us some drinks."

Candace looked around and realized that she was alone. Molly's friends, Courtney and Lindsey, were sitting on the deck on the opposite side of the pool dangling their legs in the water, skinny girls in their bikinis, surrounded by a gaggle of strange boys flexing their bare pecs. Danilo was nowhere in sight. She wandered over toward the group and heard someone say,

"What is she doing here? Please tell me she's not coming out on the boat tomorrow."

Someone else said, "Oh God, can you imagine that in a bathing suit?" Everyone laughed.

Pretending she hadn't seen them, Candace made a detour toward the bar and found a seat at the far end. There was a man nearby.

"Hey, doll, you here for the regatta?" He introduced himself as Sam. "Let me buy you a beer?"

Sam was ancient, *in his forties,* Candace thought. He was sunburned and balding, but kind of dapper in his Margaritaville shirt, flip-flops and Gap shorts that were frayed at the hems. He was also unsteady on his feet. *He seems harmless,* she thought. So she accepted the beer and took a big gulp.

"Good race, today?" Sam said.

"We just got here. I think our team is racing tomorrow," Candace said. She took another long gulp.

"What team are you with?" Sam asked.

"Do you know Nick Maguire?"

"Sure, everybody knows Nick," Sam said. "He's a regular down here every season. Actually, his boat raced in our heat today."

"Who won?" Candace asked.

"Neither of us, some crew out of New Orleans. Are you ready for another?" Sam gestured at her empty beer bottle.

Candace was shocked to see that she'd finished her entire beer. *How much time had elapsed?* She felt dizzy. "Thanks, but I should find my friends."

"I think your friends left," Sam said.

Candace frantically scanned the bar, the beach, the pool. She didn't recognize anyone. "Where did they go?"

"They got in a taxi. Don't you have a cell phone?"

"I don't have service down here," Candace said, starting to panic.

"Relax, we'll find them. Come with me."

"Um, maybe I should wait here. They'll probably be back."

"There are only two other bars on this beach. They have to be at one of them. C'mon, we can walk down by the water."

Sensing her discomfort, Sam gestured to an older woman sitting at the bar. "Judy! Jude, come here and meet . . . I forgot your name?"

"Candace."

"Right, Candace. Can I call you Candy?"

"People do," Candace said.

Judy walked over and put her arm around Sam's waist.

"This old coot bothering you, honey?" Judy said.

"No, it's fine," said Candace.

"Candy here has lost her friends and I thought we could help her find them. They must have gone down the beach," Sam said.

"Who's your friend?" Judy said.

"Nick Maguire? His sister, Molly, is my roommate at school," Candace said.

"Oh sure, everybody knows Nick, he's the kid who always has the Oxy, right?" Judy said to Sam. "C'mon, Candy, we'll help you find him."

The three of them set off walking down the beach, arm in arm, and it wasn't long before Candace heard voices that she recognized. They were coming from a dark huddle around a bonfire. The glow of the fire illuminated their faces, and Candace saw Danilo with his arms around a girl she didn't recognize. As she got closer, she saw that he had his hand inside her shorts and she was limp, maybe even unconscious. Candace suddenly felt sick and her legs buckled.

"Whoa, Candy!" said Judy. "Hang in there. Are you feeling sick? Do you need to sit down?"

"I think I need to go back to the yacht club and wait for Molly there," Candace said. "She'll probably be looking for me."

"Sure, kid," Sam said. Sam and Judy exchanged looks over Candace's head.

They escorted Candace back to the bar where she plopped down, heavily, onto a stool, buried her head in her arms and sobbed.

"It's okay, kid, your friends will come back. Don't cry." Judy rubbed Candace's back, trying to soothe her.

"Can I get you something, honey?" Sam said.

Candace lifted her head. "I want one of those rum drinks. Something sweet and sticky."

"Thatta girl, now you're talking. Rudy!" Sam waved at the bartender. "Goombay Smash for our friend Candy here."

The drink tasted like fruit juice and Candace gulped it down. As she set the empty glass down on the bar, the room suddenly seemed to get dimmer. Sam and Judy were saying something that she couldn't quite make out. It sounded like they were talking to her through a pillow.

"I need to find the bathroom," Candace said, pushing herself up on her wobbly legs. "Where is the bathroom?" Candace navigated the crowd slowly, trying not to stumble or bump into anything.

Once inside the stall, she sat on the toilet, doubled over, waiting for the room to stop spinning. It didn't, so she lay down on the floor of the stall and moaned a little as she savored the coolness of the tile. *I'll just lie here for a few minutes and then I'll feel better,* she thought. She didn't have the strength to pull herself to her knees as the nausea rolled over her. She leaned forward on her elbows and retched on the floor. Three, four times, until she was dry heaving. She heard Judy's voice outside the toilet stall.

"Are you okay, Candy? Can I come in?" Judy said.

"Um, give me a minute. I just need to lie her for another minute."

"Sam is getting us a cab, you're coming home with me," Judy said.

"Thank you," Candace said in a whisper.

The cab driver had to stop twice on the way to Judy's motel to let Candace lean out the door to puke. Finally, they pulled into the car park and Sam and Judy each took an arm and helped Candace stumble inside and onto the couch.

///

The sun shone brightly through the sliding glass door when Candace awoke.

"What time is it?" Candace said.

A voice behind her said, "Morning, sunshine, how are you feeling today?"

"Sam?" Candace said. He sounded different sober.

"It's after one. The morning racers are already back at the club. Do you want to get cleaned up and go find your friends?"

Do I? Candace wasn't sure. *They aren't really my friends, and Danilo isn't really my boyfriend.*

"Actually, I think I'd like to go home," Candace said. "Do you know where I left my luggage?"

"Rudy brought it over after he closed up last night. You left it in the check room."

"Can I get a ride to the airport? I'll wait there until I can catch a flight back to Boston," Candace said.

"I think there's a couple of flights this afternoon. Maybe to New York?" Sam said.

"Close enough!" Candace said.

//

The story Candace told everyone was that she caught a fever in the Bahamas and was rushed to the hospital and had to be medevaced back to the States.

Molly looked at her funny, but didn't press for more details. Danilo acted like nothing had ever happened. Like she had not disappeared in the Bahamas without a trace. As far as she could tell, there had been no search effort, no frantic calls to her parents. It was like she had never even been there.

Nine

CANDACE AVOIDED BEING ALONE WITH DANILO AND WAS no longer meeting him for lunch in the cafeteria or to study in the library. And he didn't seek her out. It seemed like the previous three months had never happened—as if she had imagined the whole thing. Candace checked his status updates on Facebook on a weekly basis but he wasn't very active and his relationship status remained Single.

Has he just been using me this whole time? Meanwhile all my summer clothes from last year seem too tight. Even my underwear seems too small.

"I don't understand it," Candace moaned to Molly. "I don't eat anything! What did I eat yesterday? A hard-boiled egg and an apple? Why can't I lose weight?"

"Danilo hasn't been around much lately," Molly said.

"No." Candace hesitated. *Should I tell Molly what I saw in the Bahamas, or stick with my fever story?*

"Has he said anything about the prom?" said Molly.

"I'm not sure I want to go." Candace said. "I'm too fat!"

"Oh, c'mon, it's our senior year," Molly said. "You don't want to miss the dance. Let's check out the stores on Main this afternoon."

After class, Molly and Candace walked across the Meadow toward Main Street. Candace brooded, wanting to say something to Molly about being abandoned in Nassau. *What kind of friend is she?* But she knew that Molly would deny everything and accuse Candace of being judgmental and standoffish with the Paulie girls.

Thank God it's almost over, Candace thought. *In*

two weeks I can say goodbye to all of this and never have to see any of them, ever again.

As they entered the dress shop, an older woman greeted them, about her mother's age, and Candace thought about Mommy's dress shop in Back Bay and what it would be like to have her mother wait on her. She shuddered at the thought.

"Prom dress? I'm Nancy, let me know if you need any help," the saleswoman said.

Molly made a beeline to the back of the store toward the couture display. Candace approached Nancy and lowered her voice.

"I seem to have put on some weight this semester and I'm not even sure what size I am. I need something that won't make me look fat," Candace said.

Nancy furrowed her brow. "Yes, of course. Something flattering," she said.

"Why don't you have a seat in the dressing room? Would you like some water?"

"Yes, please." Candace collapsed gratefully into the upholstered chair in the dressing room. She was surrounded by mirrors. Viewing her bulges from three sides simultaneously filled her with loathing. *I can't go to the prom looking like this,* she thought.

Nancy came in with three gowns in muted tones of blue and plum and a bottle of Poland Spring. "Your friend has found some lovely things," she said.

"Super," Candace grunted.

"Here, I brought a few ideas. Why don't you try these on and see what you think?" Nancy hung the dresses on the wall and gently shut the door.

Candace fingered the tag on a royal blue dress. *Size eighteen? Four hundred dollars? Seriously? I'll look like a beached whale,* she thought. *Why would I want to spend that kind of money on a size-eighteen dress that I'll never wear again?* Clearly she was in no mood to even think about going to any stupid prom.

Candace walked out of the dressing room without trying anything on.

"Nothing worked?" Nancy said.

"Exactly," said Candace. "But thank you for the water. Tell Molly I'll see her back at the dorm."

Candace shuffled down the path, kicking at stones and wishing she were invisible. As she approached the campus clinic, she noticed that the door was propped open and a tripod held a poster offering free STD screenings. She hesitated, then walked in.

///

Candace sat on the exam table swinging her legs to and fro as she waited for the nurse to come back with the results of her urine test.

A knock on the door and the nurse entered. Candace read her name tag: Jenny.

"Ms. Parker, I have the results of your tests. You're pregnant," Nurse Jenny said.

"Pregnant?" Candace gasped.

"Yes. Do you remember the first day of your last period?"

"Winter break," Candace said.

"February?" Nurse Jenny was fiddling with an app on her iPad.

"Yes, but I never even had sex until the first weekend in March," Candace said.

Nurse Jenny fiddled with her iPad some more. "Okay, that puts you at approximately twelve weeks. We'll schedule an ultrasound and the doctor will be able to give you a better idea of how far along you are."

Candace was silently crying.

Nurse Jenny handed her a box of tissues. "Do you want me to call someone, dear?"

Who would I call? Candace thought. *Surely not Danilo. It would be so humiliating to have to explain to him that I'm pregnant. After I told him that I was using protection. Oh, God! This is all my fault. What will Daddy say? Mommy will disown me.*

"Should I take off the patch?" Candace said, weakly.

"Patch?"

"My birth control patch," Candace said.

"Yes, you're probably overdosing on estrogen right now, which might explain the rapid weight gain," Nurse Jenny said, handing her a form. "Take this to the receptionist and she'll schedule the ultrasound. You have time to decide what you want to do. There are online support groups for pregnant teens that you should check out."

Candace shook her head. "I'm going home next week after graduation. I'd rather go to my doctor in Boston."

"That's fine," Nurse Jenny said.

///

The week flew by. While Molly and the other girls got all dolled up and went to the prom, Candace hid out in the library and watched movies on her laptop. Sara and her parents came up for graduation and Candace refused to take off her commencement gown the entire weekend, grateful for the generous folds that hid her expanding waistline. On the drive home, Daddy chattered on about Princeton while Mommy kept dropping hints about joining a gym. Candace put on her headphones to drown them out.

Where was Danilo? she brooded. *He wasn't even*

at graduation. He didn't even bother to say goodbye.
Screw him!

//

Summer in Boston was the worst, hot and humid.
Candace's thighs stuck together when she walked,
so mostly she stayed in her room, watching videos
on her computer with the window A/C unit cranked
up to high. Then she remembered Nurse Jenny
urging her to check out Facebook to find other girls.
She logged into Facebook and started searching
and quickly found a page called *Nine Months.* She
scrolled through the posts and checked out the pro-
files. Luciana was fourteen and wasn't sure who the
father was. Jasmine was a nineteen-year-old college
freshman from New Jersey. Aleecia was fifteen and
Shawna and Isabella were both eighteen and their
boyfriends were planning to marry them. Candace
scrolled past those because she knew Danilo was
never going to marry her.

Candace rested her fingers on the keyboard for several minutes while she thought about whether to post a comment. *What would I say? I'm seventeen and I've been accepted to Princeton. But I got knocked up by a guy who doesn't even care about me? I've ruined my life and I don't know how to tell my parents? Geez, what a mess!*

While she was sitting there a new post appeared.

Jasmine: "*Can I Live* is based on a true story from Nick Cannon. Check out his music video . . . "

Candace clicked on the link and started tearing up as she watched the young rapper beg his seventeen-year-old pregnant mom not to abort him. She sat back in her chair and cradled her belly.

Luciana posted a comment. "Making a big life change is scary. But you know what's even scarier? Regret."

Candace sent friend requests to all the girls on the group hoping that they would accept and she could follow them on her feed.

Ten

THE NEXT TIME CANDACE CHECKED HER FACEBOOK FEED, they were all there!

Candy: Hi! I'm 17—I'm supposed to be starting college in the fall. I got into Princeton but my parents don't know that I'm pregnant.

Aleecia: Where is the baby-daddy?

Candy: He's back in Italy with his family. He doesn't know.

Shawna: You gotta tell him, girl! He should step up.

Candy: I doubt it. He's already moved on. We haven't really talked since spring break.

Isabella: Tell your parents. Today. Let me know what happens.

Suddenly her bedroom door opened and Julia, their Jamaican housekeeper, poked her head in.

"Hey, you could knock?" Candace immediately regretted her tone. *Why am I so irritable?* she wondered.

"I did knock, Miss Candace," Julia said. "You don't hear me with those headphones. Your mother sent me to fetch you for dinner. Come and eat."

Dinner at the Parker home was a formal affair. Daddy and Mommy sat stiffly at opposite ends of the dining room table, which Julia polished to a high sheen every Thursday afternoon. Candace and Sara took their places and sat with their hands in their laps while Julia set their plates in front of them. Candace glumly surveyed her ration of broccoli and steamed salmon, while eyeing the mound of mashed potatoes on Sara's plate. If she was going to get any of those she was going to have to spill the news. They wouldn't starve a fetus, would they?

"In other news . . . " Candace said.

"What is it, Candace?" Mommy said, not looking up from her plate.

Sara was looking at Candace curiously.

"I'm going to have a baby," Candace said. "Can I have some mashed potatoes?"

Daddy put his glass down hard on the table, the water sloshing over the edge to form a puddle. Mommy's knife clattered onto her plate. She appeared to deflate into her chair. They looked at each other. Nobody looked at Candace—including Sara, who stared down at her mound of mashed potatoes.

"You're pregnant?" Mommy said at last.

"Wow. That is big news," Daddy said.

"That boy!" Mommy said. "Danilo, right?"

"Yes, but he doesn't know. Like you said, Mommy, he's gone and I'm never going to see him again. Can I puh-lease have some mashed potatoes? I'm eating for two here," Candace said.

Julia looked at Mommy for approval and walked to the kitchen to retrieve the bowl of potatoes. She set it in front of Candace, who helped herself to a generous serving.

"I'll make an appointment with Dr. Bird in the

morning," Mommy said. "I believe she performs abortions." She went back to picking at her salmon.

"I'm keeping the baby," Candace said. "I've decided."

"Whoa," Daddy said. "That's a big decision. Shouldn't we talk about this? About your future? What about Princeton?"

Candace had already thought about that. *Surely Princeton accepts mothers? The housing options were single, double, four-person suite. Where did they house the mothers with babies?*

"I don't think you've thought this through, Candace," Mommy said. "Come to the doctor with me and we'll talk about it."

"I didn't pay private school tuition for you to fuck around and get yourself knocked up," Daddy shouted and pounded the table, spilling more water.

"George! Not in front of Sara!" Mommy said.

Candace was starting to feel the first stirrings of life in her belly. She visualized, with some sense of pleasure, a swarthy little toad with a full head of coarse, curly hair inside her. She was thinking of naming him Squirt. Or Bean Sprout. She imagined she could feel him coiling on his hind legs to leap against the walls of her womb, bashing his little bug-eyed head into her again and again. It made her giggle. And it made her wet her pants a little.

"Candace?" Daddy was looking at her with a worried expression. "You're not saying anything. And you have an odd look on your face. Are you feeling okay? Do you need to lie down?"

"I'm fine, Daddy."

As Candace finished the pile of mashed potatoes and slouched in her dining chair cradling her belly in her hands, her parents exchanged startled looks.

//

After dinner, Candace rushed back upstairs to check in on Facebook.

Candy: I told my parents!

Isabella: And? Girl, don't keep us in suspense!

Candy: My mother is going to call her gyno to schedule an abortion.

Aleecia: They can't make you do that!

Candy: I know. But how am I supposed to have a baby and go to college?

Jasmine: People do it.

Shawna: Sharon Osborne says having an abortion was the worst thing she ever did.

Candace checked out Danilo's Facebook and saw that he had changed his profile photo. He had his arm around a tall blonde girl in a tiny bikini. It looked like they were on a boat in the Mediterranean.

Well that's just peaches, isn't it? Goodbye, Danilo!

///

The next morning, Mommy drove Candace to the Women's Health Center on Route 9 in Brookline.

"How did we get an appointment so soon?" Candace said.

"I told them that you were further along and

that we couldn't wait too long for the abortion,"
Mommy said,

"I don't want kill Squirt," Candace said.

"Who?"

"I can feel him, I don't want to kill him," Candace said.

"Oh, dear," Mommy said.

In the examination room, Candace lay on the table as Dr. Bird squeezed some cold gel onto her belly and ran the ultrasound wand in circles up and around her lower abdomen.

"Eek, that's cold!" Candace said.

Dr. Bird turned the monitor toward Candace's head. "Do you want to see the baby?" she asked.

"No!" said Mommy. "We came in to get an abortion."

"We don't do abortions here," said Dr. Bird. "I can refer you to a clinic."

"I want to see Squirt," Candace said.

"She keeps calling it Squirt . . . I don't know," Mommy said, shaking her head.

Dr. Bird pressed the wand against Candace's

abdomen and pointed to the monitor. "Here's the heartbeat. That's pretty much all you can see at this stage. You're what, about sixteen weeks? Come back in a month and we'll be able to see fingers and toes and determine the sex."

"How do you determine the sex?" Candace asked.

"Well, if we see a penis—it's a boy," Dr. Bird said. "It's kind of obvious."

"Oh, good grief," Mommy said.

Dr. Bird wiped the goop off of Candace's abdomen. "Why don't you come into my office and let's talk," she said.

Dr. Bird's office was small and Mommy and Candace sat elbow-to-elbow facing her across a cluttered desk.

"Candace," Dr. Bird said. "There's still time for you to consider your options. Abortion is still an option. Adoption is another option. If you choose to abort, it will take a few weeks for your body to eliminate the hormones and then you'll start to feel like yourself again. But carrying a baby to term will have a profound affect on your body and your mental health."

"I want to keep it," Candace said.

"So I guess it's adoption," said Mommy.

"I said I'm keeping it!" Candace said.

"You have a few months to think about that, Candace. Keep your options open. Don't forget about Princeton," Mommy said. "Your father will never forgive you."

Princeton again. Dammit.

//

Back at home, Candace locked herself in her room and pulled up the Princeton website. On the page for new admissions she saw a button that said "Request Deferral." She stared at the page and just then, Squirt leapt, bashing his curly little head against her bladder. She felt her panties get damp.

"Okay, kid," Candace said. "I get it." She clicked on the button.

She logged onto Facebook and posted.

Candy: I deferred college.

Jasmine: No!

Shawna: Me too. I'll go back at night I guess.

Candy: My parents want me to give the baby up.

Isabella: Everything in your life is a reflection of a choice you have made. If you want a different result, make a different choice. | 28 people liked this.

Eleven

CANDACE WAS AT TARGET SHOPPING FOR BABY SUPPLIES. Her cart was stuffed with a portable crib and mattress, diapers, bottles, a collapsible stroller, and a BabyBjorn.

"Candy, hi!"

Candace spun around to see Sonya and Emily, two friends from Brookline.

They were pushing baskets loaded with comforters, pillows, notebooks, calculators, and batteries.

"College shopping?" Candace asked weakly.

"Yeah! Crazy huh?" Emily said. "My mom gave me her credit card. Look at this loot!"

"Princeton, right?" Sonya said. "I saw your Facebook."

Damn. Candace suddenly realized she needed to update her status.

"I deferred my admission," she said. "I'm taking a gap year." *More like a baby gap year,* she thought.

"Wow! Are you going to be volunteering someplace exciting?" Emily said.

Seeing the cart piled with baby supplies, Sonya asked, "Are you going to be working with children? That would be awesome!"

"Where are you going?" Candace changed the subject.

"Cornell," they said in unison.

"Pre-med," said Emily.

"Hotel management," said Sonya.

"Awesome," said Candace without enthusiasm. "Well, gotta go."

"Great seeing you, Candy! Let's grab brunch before we leave," said Emily.

"Sure!" said Candace. "Definitely." She steered her cart away from the checkout counters and into the deepest reaches of the menswear section, hoping Sonya and Emily would be checking out and leaving soon. She parked her cart behind a tall display of hoodie sweatshirts and sat on the edge of a counter stacked with Levi's.

"That was awkward," she said to Squirt. She had been talking to him a lot lately. "I'm so lonely," she said, tears stinging her eyes. "You are my only companion, and by the way, you're a good listener," she said as she caressed her belly. "I really appreciate that you never argue with me or insult me with cutting comments like Mommy does. I'm sorry I didn't introduce you; that was rude, I know. I'm not ashamed; I'm really not. But to tell you the truth, I wish that was me—us—sorry, packing for college. And it's not your fault that I'm deferring a year. I don't want you to ever feel guilty about ruining my life. I mean you're not ruining my life. I'm doing that just fine by myself."

She looked up and saw him. "Oh shit! Sorry, Squirt—language. You're not going to believe who is here. What is he doing here? In Target?"

Danilo was browsing in the men's underwear

section. In a panic, Candace abandoned her cart and started to walk in the opposite direction.

"Candace?"

"Fuck, he's spotted us! Sorry again, Squirt."

Candace took a hoodie off the rack and held it up like a curtain in front of her. "Danilo? Fancy meeting you here. In Target. Aren't you supposed to be in Italy?"

"Change of plans. My father made me apply to a bunch of American schools and I got into Boston College. So here I am," he said. "He thinks it will be easier for me to find a job on Wall Street if I have an American diploma."

"No shit! Sorry," she whispered in the general direction of her belly button. "So you'll be going to college two miles from where I live?"

"Well, yeah, but you'll be at Princeton. New Jersey, right?"

"Uh, right!"

"So how are you?" he said. "You look great— your hair so shiny and your skin, what's the word? Luminous!"

Candace was taken aback. She had forgotten how free he was with the compliments. That Italian upbringing.

"Thank you, you look nice, too. Didn't I see on Facebook that you had a girlfriend? Lots of pictures of her."

"Ah yes, another reason my father banished me to this forsaken backwater. He didn't approve. Her family wasn't quite at our level," he said.

"Well, then he probably wouldn't approve of me, either?" she said.

"No, of course not."

Wow. That stings! At that moment, Candace made a pact with Squirt that Danilo was never going to know about him, was never going to be able to hurt him or reject him or tell him that he wasn't at the right level. *Screw you! Sorry, Squirt,* she thought.

"Well I really need to get going. It was nice to see you." Candace was still holding the stupid hoodie in front of herself, hoping Danilo would turn and walk away so she could hide until he, too, had left the store. *Memo to self,* Candace thought, *avoid Target on back-to-school sale days.* He was still standing there. *What now?* "You must have lots of shopping to do? Ba-bye now," she said.

"This shitty store? No, I don't shop here."

Really, then what were you doing in the underwear section, fingering the boxers and briefs? Candace hoped that Squirt could read her thoughts. *What a phony!*

"Okay, then," she said, tossing the hoodie onto the Levi display. "See ya." She retrieved her basket and navigated it to the checkout counter. *Screw everyone. Sorry, Squirt,* she thought.

///

When she got home, she logged onto Facebook.

Candy: I saw my baby-daddy in Target!

Luciana: OMG! Did he see you?

Candy: Yeah, but he didn't seem to notice my baby bump. I tried to hide it.

Jasmine: You didn't tell him?

Candy: He said some shit about me not being good enough for his family.

Luciana: That's just fucked up!

Candy: I know, right?

Aleecia: Am I the only girl who feels alone? It seems like my friends prefer to not think I'm pregnant. Nobody invites me to hang out anymore.

Candy: You're not the only one. I saw my BFFs at Target too. They were shopping for dorm stuff.

Shawna: Once the baby is here you won't be alone.

//

"Mommy, what's *la mas* class?" Candace asked one morning at breakfast.

"Look it up on the Google," Mommy said. She didn't look up from her newspaper.

"You mean, Google it?" Sara asked, giggling.

"Whatever!" Mommy said. Sara went to find her iPad.

Mommy glared at Candace. "Where did you hear about that?"

"There was a pregnant lady in line in front of me at Target and she said something to her husband about *la mas* class. Is that Spanish for something?"

Sara came back into the kitchen. "How do you spell it?"

"It's Lamaze," Mommy said. "L-a-m-a-z-e. They teach women how to give birth."

Candace's eyes widened. "How do you do it?"

"Look," Mommy said. "Your body knows what to do. But it is very painful and scary. Lamaze teaches you what to expect and how to get through it."

Sara was busy swiping her iPad.

"Oh, here it is. Here it is," she said. "There's a class at Brigham and Women's in Longwood. We can walk there. Let's sign up!"

"Both of us?" asked Candace.

"You need a partner, a coach," said Mommy. "Usually it's the father, but it can be a sister or a friend. Whoever is going to be there in the delivery room with you."

"Me, me, me. Pick me," said Sara. She bounced up and down in her chair. "I wanna be the coach!"

"Okay," said Candace. "Sign us up."

Sara swiped and clicked on her iPad and held out her hand. "Credit card, Mommy."

Mommy sighed. "Bring me my purse."

Sara dashed into the study.

"Sara!" Mommy yelled. "Don't run in the house—you sound like a herd of elephants."

Sara came tiptoeing back into the kitchen with Mommy's wallet.

Mommy dug out her Visa card and handed it to Sara.

Sara clicked and swiped some more. "We have two choices," she said. "Saturday morning at ten or Sunday evening at six. I'm thinking Saturday."

"Agreed," Candace said.

Sara clicked once more. "Done!" she said.

Twelve

ON SATURDAY MORNING, THE GIRLS WENT DOWN TO breakfast dressed in sweat pants and T-shirts.

"Going to the gym?" asked Daddy.

"Lamaze class," said Sara.

"What the fuck?" Daddy exclaimed. "Lois, did you know about this?"

"Don't look at me," Mommy said. "Sara signed them up."

"Sara?" Daddy's voice dripped with sarcasm. "She has a credit card? Sara is now making the financial decisions for the family?"

"She used my credit card," said Mommy.

"Of course she did, Lois," Daddy said.

"Can we discuss this later?" Mommy asked.

"Oh yes, we'll talk about it later," Daddy said.

Sara and Candace scooted out the back door.

"Geez, what was that about?" Sara asked.

"Get used to it, kid," Candace said. "Daddy is all about the money."

//

Candace and Sarah found their way to the common room at the hospital.

Inside, couples sat in a circle on a large mat. The women sat in front of their partners and leaned against them. The girls took an open spot with Sara sitting behind, supporting Candace's back.

"Hey fatty, not so much pressure," Sara hissed.

"Shut up!" Candace hissed back.

"Welcome to our class!" the instructor said. "I'm Joanne. I'm a registered maternity nurse here at Brigham and Women's."

"Hello, Joanne," the group said in unison.

"It looks like we have some newcomers today,"

Joanne said. "Would you like to introduce your-selves?"

"Nope," Candace muttered.

"Hi, everybody," Sara said. "This is Candace." She pointed at Candace. "And I'm her sister, Sara. I'm the coach."

"Welcome, Candace and Sara," Joanne said. "You've already figured out the sitting position. Now why are we sitting this way? When our mommies go into labor, the coaches will help them bend forward and push. Now, let's practice our breathing again. Four deep breaths, panting. And then one slow breath. Whoo, whoo, whoo, whoo. Close your teeth. Ssssss. Now, all together. Contraction!"

The coaches and mommies leaned forward, look-ing at their toes. Collectively, the group panted in unison.

"Woo, woo, woo, woo, sssss," Candace panted. "What the fuck is this?"

"I don't know," Sara said. "This helps the baby come out?"

"In what way does this help the baby come out?" Candace asked.

"Just shut up and follow Joanne's instructions," Sara said. "We'll get the hang of this."

//

Back at home, Candace checked in with her posse.

Candy: Anybody check out this Lamaze thing?

Aleecia: Kyle and me go every Saturday.

Candy: So what's the deal?

Shawna: Something about natural childbirth. You can google it.

Izzy: So if we just do this breathing thing, the baby pops out? Just like that?

Jasmine: I guess, right?

//

"Mommy, I don't feel good," Candace said one morning at breakfast. At least now, she was allowed to eat a real breakfast—eggs, toast, cereal, whatever she wanted—as long as it was organic and healthy for the baby.

"In what way?" Mommy asked. "You haven't had morning sickness in quite a while, are you feeling nauseous?"

"No. When I walk, or ride on the T, my insides feel heavy and it hurts when they bounce."

Mommy thought for a minute. "Hmm, I don't remember feeling that when I was pregnant. Why don't we make an appointment with Dr. Bird? She'll probably want to do another ultrasound."

Candace perked up. She was dying to see Squirt again! Maybe this time she would see his nose and his fingers and toes and maybe his penis! "Can we go today?"

"Don't be silly. We'll be lucky if we can get an appointment this week," Mommy said. "How are you doing on the paper?"

Daddy had enrolled Candace in two classes through the Harvard extension program. Daddy chose The Ancient Greek Hero to make sure she was keeping her mind *active and engaged*. Those were his words. Candace selected Existentialism: Existence and Anxiety because it sounded funny.

"I'm halfway through *The Iliad*. I keep falling asleep," Candace said.

"It's important that you demonstrate to Princeton that you've made good use of this gap year. You don't want them to rescind the offer, now do you?"

"They can do that?"

"You bet they can," Mommy said. "If word ever gets out that you got yourself pregnant and wasted a year, you might find it hard to get accepted into any school, including UMass."

Candace was pretty sure that Mommy was lying. She knew Mommy was worried that she would lose her ambition and would never leave home. *Kids were doing that, these days*, she thought—*living at home into their 30s. That wasn't an option here.* She knew Mommy and Daddy had other plans for their golden years.

"Get your fanny upstairs and finish that book."

Candace heard an edge in Mommy's voice and didn't argue.

//

Dr. Bird had a worried look on her face. She passed the wand over the same spot on Candace's swollen abdomen repeatedly, pressing harder each time.

"Ow," Candace said. "I think I need to pee."

"Bear with me, sweetie," Dr. Bird said. "One more pass and . . . okay, that's it." She snapped off her latex gloves and looked up at Mommy. "We have a situation here."

"What kind of situation?" Candace was scared. "Is Squirt okay?"

"Would you stop calling him that?" Mommy spat.

"Everyone calm down," Dr. Bird said. Her voice fell an octave into a soothing tone. "Let's go into my office."

Candace gingerly lowered herself into the hard chair in Dr. Bird's office. When everyone was settled,

Dr. Bird said, "It seems that the uterine wall hasn't developed as it should. The wall is quite thin—paper-thin in fact. The danger is that the baby could puncture the wall with a kick. That could lead to an infection, or worse."

"Why? What caused this?" Mommy asked.

"This condition appears in fewer than one percent of pregnancies. Could be a hormonal imbalance, or the position of the uterus can sometimes cause low blood flow. There are medications we can try but the side effects are risky. The safest course of action is to put Candace on bed rest and hope for the best."

"Bed rest? What does that mean?" Candace asked.

"You'll need to stay in bed, flat on your back or your side, for the next two months—the rest of your term. No walking, no sitting up. We can't have any pressure on the uterine wall. Only get up to use the bathroom and for monthly doctor visits. Nothing else. At this point, my dear, you are a human incubator. If you want this baby to be born, you need to lie still and let him grow."

"Him? Squirt's a boy?" Candace said excitedly.

"Oh yes, I forgot to tell you. It's a boy."

"Can I have a picture?"

Dr. Bird printed out a grainy black-and-white screen shot from her computer.

Candace clutched the photo. She could see Squirt's head in profile and he appeared to be sucking his thumb. *My baby! Bed rest won't be so bad,* she thought, on the drive home. *No more stupid Harvard Extension classes. Maybe I will start a blog, or take up painting. Better yet, knitting. I could learn to knit!* She was excited about the possibilities and was glad the hurting would stop. *I will be the best incubator ever!*

//

As soon as she got home, she logged onto Facebook.

Candy: I'm on bed rest for two months!

Jasmine: What does that mean?

Candy: I have to stay in bed. If I get up and walk around I might lose the baby.

Isabella: That sucks.

Thirteen

THAT NIGHT CANDACE AWOKE TO THE SOUND OF HER PARENTS ARGUING. SHE COULD TELL THEY WERE TRYING TO keep their voices low but the intensity resonated through the plaster walls. She couldn't make out the words but they were short, emphatic statements, each one louder than the one before. Then Candace thought she heard a slap. *Flesh on flesh violence, fuck! The last time they did this was when I got accepted into St. Paul's. It was Daddy's idea to send me to boarding school, hoping to improve my chances of getting into Princeton. But Mommy said they couldn't afford it. They fought about it for months. I never wanted to go there—I didn't want to leave my friends. But in the end, I was glad to get away from all the fighting.*

Candace felt sick.

//

In the morning, Sara brought Candace her breakfast tray.

"Where is Julia?"

Sara sat down on the bed. "Mommy sent her home. Too much dirty laundry being aired, she said."

Candace bit into an English muffin. "Why, what's going on down there?" she said with her mouth full.

"Sorry," she said after she had swallowed. "What's going on?"

"Daddy is moving out."

"What? Why?" Candace started to cry.

Sara started to cry too. "Mommy says it's your fault. Daddy wants you to get an abortion and he says Mommy is coddling you."

"Coddling me?" *Mommy has been nothing but abusive to me*, Candace thought.

"Taking you to doctor appointments. He thinks she's been encouraging you."

"Encouraging me? Yeah, right!" Candace's voice dripped with sarcasm. "It's clear that everyone wants Squirt dead. They want us to go away. But I love him. He's my baby. And he loves me, I can tell. I can!"

"Mommy didn't even cry," Sara said, sobbing. "She just announced that her husband of twenty years was leaving and she didn't shed a tear."

"Where is Daddy going to live?" Candace asked.

"He's staying at the Marriott in Coolidge Corner until he finds an apartment," Sara said. "Can I lie down?"

Candace scooted over to make room and Sara lay down beside her and spooned her sister with her body. "Can I feel the baby?" Sara said.

Candace took Sara's arm and wrapped it around her belly. Just then Squirt did a somersault and both of the girls shrieked and giggled. Then they lay there quietly for a while hoping for another kick.

"He didn't even come up to say good-bye?" Candace asked, quietly whimpering.

"I don't think he wants to see you," Sara said in a whisper.

"Now they both hate me," Candace said.

"When can you get out of bed?" Sara asked.

"At thirty-eight weeks. If Squirt can wait until thirty-eight weeks, he'll be full-term and it will be safe to get up. One more month of hell."

"Do you want me to bring you something to read?" Sara asked.

"No, I just want to go back to sleep and hope that when I wake up that this was all a bad dream."

When Sara had left, Candace opened up her laptop.

Candy: My parents are getting a divorce because of me.

Shawna: My mom says my dad left because of me. She wants me to move out.

Luciana: Tomorrow will be better. The struggle you're in today is developing the strength you need for tomorrow.

Candy: Where do you get these quotes?

Luciana: Quotesberry.com. Check it out.

//

There was a knock on the door. "Candace, are you awake?"

Candace moaned and rolled over.

Mommy knocked harder. "Candace, unlock this door!"

Candace opened the door and then fell back onto the bed, her back to Mommy.

"When was the last time you showered? It reeks in here." Mommy opened a window. "Candace, I've had enough of this. You've destroyed our family and I think it's time to put an end to this drama."

"You can't force me to have an abortion," Candace said into her pillow.

"It's too late for that, young lady. Now, your only option is adoption. I made an appointment with an agency that comes highly recommended. There are lots of loving couples out there who desperately want a child."

"I'm not supposed to get out of bed," Candace said.

"You are allowed to get up for your doctor appointments. I'm sure you can make it to this appointment."

Candace moaned.

"Daddy's not coming back unless you give up the baby," Mommy said.

"Daddy is coming back?" Candace asked, craning her neck to look at Mommy.

"Only if you give up the baby. We want our family back; we want our life back. The way it used to be. You'll start college next fall and we'll all be able to put this behind us."

Candace cradled her engorged belly and began to weep. *What a horrible choice. Between her family and, well, her family. Her baby. I have to abandon my baby to salvage my parents' marriage. What is this, Sophie's Choice? That was too much to ask.*

"Mommy, please?"

"Candace you're worn out. You're not thinking straight. Julia said you've stopped eating. You're weak; you're emotional. Remember what Dr. Bird said about carrying the baby to full-term would do to your emotions? Well, here we are. You've got to think logically about this. You're not ready to be a mother, and God knows I'm not ready to be a grandmother!"

Candace was worn out. Bed rest felt like solitary confinement. Locked in her room for months on end with only Squirt and her Facebook friends for company. A food tray delivered to her cell three times a day. She had lost track of days and even whether it was day or night. She was sleeping twenty hours a day, comforting herself in the knowledge that she was being a good incubator. A human incubator for Squirt. *After all this effort, she was supposed to sacrifice the baby?*

"Mommy," Candace rolled over and faced her mother defiantly. "This isn't about you, and it's not about Daddy. If Daddy left because he doesn't want you to take care of me—well that's just fucked up. Sorry, Mommy, but that's just wrong."

"Candace, don't be impertinent. The appointment is at two. Get up and take a shower. I'll send Julia up to help you."

//

Julia poked her head inside the door a few minutes later and gasped. Candace had emptied her closet onto the floor and lay curled up in a ball on her bed.

"Candace, what is it?" Julia said.

"Mommy forgot one little detail," Candace said morosely. "I have nothing to wear. Nothing fits! Am I supposed to go out there looking like a homeless person in a T-shirt and a bathrobe?"

"Oh, my!" Julia said. "That won't do." She hurried downstairs.

Candace heard Julia and Mommy arguing. Then she heard Julia's heavy breathing as she mounted the stairs again.

"Okay," Julia said, out of breath.

"Julia, sit down."

Julia sat at Candace's desk. "Okay," she started again. "Your mother said to go to Amazon on your computer and order something pretty from the maternity store. She said Amazon has same-day delivery. Imagine that!"

"What about the two o'clock appointment?" Candace asked.

"She's calling the agency to reschedule. I'll clean up this mess while you take a shower."

Candace logged onto Amazon and scrolled through maternity dresses, pants, tops, underwear, yoga outfits, and bathing suits. Suddenly, she was having fun. She put two pairs of skinny stretch pants and two pretty blouses into her shopping cart along with a fleece tracksuit, a bra and some panties and then tossed in a pink nightgown-robe combo to wear in the hospital. She clicked on same-day delivery and checked her email for the confirmation. Ping! Her package would arrive by three p.m.

Candace stood in the shower for a long time,

lathering her hair three times to remove two weeks worth of accumulated grease. When she was clean she filled up the tub and soaked in the hot water. She shaved her legs for the first time in months. Candace was in heaven. She wrapped herself in a giant towel and waddled back to her room. Julia had picked up all the clothes and made the bed with fresh sheets. The window was cracked open and the air in the room was cold and refreshing.

///

Candace looked quite fetching in her new clothes, her hair golden and shiny. Tears sprang to Mommy's eyes. "My goodness, Candace, you look lovely—like a ripe melon. I should have thought of this earlier. You'll make a great impression at the agency. Your baby should be in high demand."

Candace bit her lip and didn't take the bait. She was just happy to have new clothes and underwear that fit.

Fourteen

IN THE LOBBY OF THE BOSTON ADOPTION AGENCY, THE walls were lined with photos of happy couples holding babies—older couples, gay couples. Candace wondered why there were no photos of young couples. Candace caressed her belly and tried to imagine the people in the photos taking Squirt home from the hospital. "I won't let them take you," she whispered.

They were ushered into an office. The plate on the door read, *Madeleine Schlosser, LICSW*. A heavyset older woman in a wrinkled maroon pantsuit approached them with her hand extended. Her hair looked like she had just rolled out of bed and she wore no makeup. "Mrs. Parker?" she said to Mommy. "We spoke on the phone."

Mommy shook her hand and gestured toward Candace. "This is my daughter, Candace."

"Have a seat, you two," Madeleine said.

Madeleine leaned forward, her elbows on the desk, hands folded under her chin as if she were about to say a prayer. "So you want to give your baby up for adoption?"

Candace started to say, "No," but Mommy interrupted.

"Yes."

"Candace, doll, do you know who the father is?" Madeleine asked.

"Yes," Candace replied.

"Do you know where he is?" Madeleine asked.

Mommy started to say, "No," but this time Candace interrupted.

"Yes," Candace said.

"You do?" Mommy asked, surprised. "I thought he went back to Europe."

"Europe?" Madeleine said. "Oh, this could get complicated. Where is he?"

"He's a freshman at Boston College," Candace said.

"What?" Mommy shrieked. "Have you been in touch with him?"

"Not really," Candace said. "I ran into him at Target a few months ago. He doesn't even know about Squirt."

"Squirt?" Madeleine asked.

"Oh, good God," Mommy said. "That's her pet name for the baby. Ridiculous!"

Madeleine took a deep breath and sat back in her chair. "Okay, let's start at the beginning. Tell me about the father. Birth fathers have rights in the state of Massachusetts. And he's European?"

"He's Italian," Candace said.

"Italy? The court system there is medieval. I don't think our in-house council is qualified to take this case. We'll have to hire a specialist."

"How much will that cost?" Mommy asked, her voice rising in alarm.

"Oh, you don't need to worry, the adopting family pays all of our fees." Madeleine said. "But this case is starting to sound quite complicated. Candace, the birth father—what's his name?"

"Danilo Rossi," Candace said.

"Danilo?" Madeleine repeated. "Candace, Danilo has rights. We'll need to have his written termination of parental rights. Our families need to know that the father won't be coming back to assert his parental rights at some point. It's our policy."

"What if we go back to the beginning and say that we don't know who the father is?" Mommy suggested.

Madeleine raised her eyebrows. "Mrs. Parker, I am licensed by the state of Massachusetts. I can't un-hear what you've already told me. Candace, doll, you're going to have to contact Danilo and get his signature before we can move forward with the adoption."

"I don't want to give Squirt away," Candace said.

"What?" Madeleine squawked. "That's a whole new kettle of fish. You're not choosing adoption?"

"No," Candace said. "Mommy is forcing me."

"You don't understand," Mommy interjected. "My husband left me. The choice is adoption or divorce."

"Heavens to Betsy, we've got quite a mess here," Madeleine exclaimed. Then she folded her hands again and rested them on the desk. "Here at the Boston Adoption Agency, we only deal with voluntary adoptions. The birth mother and father both voluntarily waive their parental rights, the adopting family agrees to whatever adoption plan the birth parents choose—closed or open. One hundred percent customer satisfaction. That's our policy."

Madeleine rose. "Ladies, thank you for coming in today. I'm sorry we couldn't be of service." She gestured toward the door.

//

Mommy was fuming as she unlocked the passenger door of the Subaru. Candace buckled her seat belt and Mommy exploded. "Now you've gone and done it! You've ruined everything."

"Mommy, I'm sorry," Candace said. She began to cry.

"What am I going to tell your father?"

Candace thought for a minute. "Tell him that the Italian legal system is medieval and we have to hire a special attorney. That will cost thousands of dollars. You know Daddy. He'll freak."

Mommy started laughing in a weird, kind of hysterical way.

//

The next afternoon, Candace was dozing in her bed when Daddy knocked on her door.

"Candace, can I come in?"

"The door's open," she mumbled, pulling herself up slightly on the pillows to face him.

"Hi, Daddy. Are you moving back in?"

"Why is it so dark in here?" Daddy tugged at

the curtains and dragged the desk chair over next to the bed to sit down. "Candace, your mother called me and told me about the meeting with the adoption agency yesterday. I think I need to speak with Danilo."

Candace's eyes widened. "Talk to Danilo about what?"

Daddy frowned. "We need to resolve this. Is he going to step up and be a father, or is he going to waive his rights? Nobody will adopt the baby if there is a chance that Danilo will appear at some time in the future to claim it."

"How will you find him?" Candace asked.

"I want you to text him and tell him to meet you at the Panera Bread in Coolidge Corner. You arrange a time with him and I'll meet him there." Daddy handed Candace her cell phone. "Right now," he said. "See if he can meet you today."

"What should I say?" Candace asked, her voice quivering.

"Geez, Candace! Just say hi and see if he responds," Daddy said, exasperated.

Candace texted, hi.

They waited.

A few minutes went by and then: hi kid. Wassup?

Candace started giggling. *This is fun,* she thought—*like being in a detective movie.*

She texted, I need 2 talk 2 u. Meet me at panera in coolidge corner

"What's he saying?" Daddy hissed.

"Wait!" Candace hissed back.

Danilo replied, sure. When?

Candace texted, today?

Danilo replied, 5 ok?

Candace texted, Yesss

Candace's head fell back on the pillow, a beatific smile on her face.

"What happened?" Daddy said.

"Meet him there at five o'clock."

//

Daddy ordered an iced tea and found a table near the

front door. At few minutes after five, he saw Danilo get off the T and cross the street, walking north on Harvard Street.

Little bastard, Daddy thought. *He's ruined my family, my marriage, my life.*

Danilo pulled open the glass door and Daddy waved, calling out, "Danilo!"

Danilo did a double take and then smiled, "Hi, Mr. Parker. I'm meeting Candace here."

"She couldn't make it," Daddy said. "She's confined to bed."

A cloud passed over Danilo's face. "Is she hurt? Is she okay?"

"Sit down," Daddy said.

Danilo pulled over a chair from a neighboring table and sat with a worried expression on his face.

Fifteen

"CANDACE IS PREGNANT," DADDY SAID. "TELL ME YOU didn't know that?"

Danilo looked completely panicked. "No! I saw her in August at the mall and she looked perfectly fine! She didn't say anything."

Danilo held his head in his hands. Then he looked up. "How do you know it's mine?"

Daddy grunted. "We'd be happy to order a paternity test, but she's due in December. Looks like she got pregnant in early March. That's when you started dating, right?"

"She told me she had protection!" Danilo protested. "I offered to buy condoms, but she said it was okay."

"You didn't use a condom?" Daddy shouted. "You irresponsible little piece of shit!"

People three tables away turned to look at them.

Danilo started to cry. "Mr. Parker, I'm sorry, I didn't know. She never told me."

Daddy slid a legal document across the table toward Danilo.

"We're giving the baby up for adoption and I need you to sign this document," Daddy said. "You need to waive your parental rights."

"What does that mean?" Danilo asked.

"You're giving up responsibility for the child, including your obligation to pay child support. You'll agree to never see the child, ever."

"No, no," Danilo said, pushing the paper back toward Daddy. "My parents would never forgive me. I need to call my father."

"What is wrong with you kids?" Daddy said angrily. "Why don't you want to just get back to living your own life?"

"What are you saying?"

"Candace refused to have an abortion and now

she's refusing adoption," Daddy said. "She's eighteen. She has her whole life ahead of her, and she wants to keep the baby. She should be at college. Instead she's lying in bed waiting to go into labor."

"Why is she in bed?" Danilo said. "Is she sick?"

"Some complication with the uterus. She can't get up until the baby is full-term," Daddy said.

"Can I see her?"

"Oh, good God!" Daddy said. "Are you telling me you care about her, or this baby? Where have you been for the last six months?"

Danilo stood up, shoving his chair backward. "I'm telling you, I didn't know! If I'm going to be a father, she should have told me." Danilo slammed his fist on the table and stormed out of the restaurant.

Out on the street, he texted Candace: can I speak to you?

Candace replied, Daddy told you?

He texted, yes. Can I come over?

She replied, give me an hour? I need to take a shower.

He texted, ok.

"Julia!" Candace shouted. "Julia, I need help."

Julia came puffing up the stairs. "What is it?"

"He's coming over. I need to clean up. Can you change the sheets while I take a shower and change?"

"He, who?" asked Julia.

"Danilo is coming over—in one hour! I don't want him to see me like this," Candace said. "We need to hurry!"

"Mr. Danilo is coming here?" Julia said. "We need to clean the place! Hop in the shower, Miss Candace."

Candace rushed through her shower and dried her hair with a towel. Julia had changed the sheets and opened the drapes and the windows. She even had sprayed the room with Fabreze and it smelled vaguely of wildflowers. Candace pulled her hospital outfit out of the dresser and yanked off the tags. Tugging the nightgown over her head, she admired in the mirror the way her engorged breasts filled out the low-cut bodice. Julia plumped up the pillows and Candace carefully lowered herself into position.

At seven twenty-two, Danilo texted, I'm outside.

She replied, ring the bell. Julia will let you in.

The bell rang. Candace was a bundle of nerves. She was terrified to face him after all this time. *What is he going to say?* She heard Julia greet Danilo and direct him upstairs. She heard him on the stairs and then he stopped. Of course, he had never been up here before, he didn't know where her room was.

"Danilo?" she called out. "In here."

He appeared in the doorway. His jaw was set.

Danilo has filled out a bit since I last saw him, she thought.

"Surprise," she said, trying to lighten up the atmosphere.

He walked over to her and stood next to the bed. "Surprise? Seriously? What the fuck were you thinking?"

"Danilo. . ." she stammered.

"You said you had protection! You lied to me? What—to trick me? Am I supposed to marry you, now? Was that the plan?"

"There was no plan," she said. "I was a virgin. I was stupid. I made a mistake."

"Okay, so why didn't you get an abortion?" Danilo demanded. "That's what all the other girls do."

"Like the girl in the Bahamas?"

Danilo looked confused. "What girl?"

"I saw you with that girl on the beach," Candace said.

"You were there?" he asked. "I thought you got sick and flew home?"

"I flew home the next day," Candace said. "I was on the beach looking for Molly and the other girls and I saw you with her. And then when we got back to school, it was over. You just stopped talking to me."

"Look, I was never really all that into you," he said. "It was the end of senior year. Time to move on. I didn't know you were pregnant!"

"Wow," she said. "So here we are."

He took a step closer. "Can I sit down?"

She nodded and Danilo sat down on the side of the bed. "Am I hurting you?" he asked.

"No," she said with a grimace.

"Can I touch it?" he said, his eyes glued to her belly.

Candace took Danilo's hand and pressed it to her abdomen. "He's kicking."

Danilo jumped when he felt the baby move. "Shit! He hates me!"

"How did you know that it's a boy?" Candace asked.

"It's a boy?" Danilo said. "What's his name?"

"Sq—", Candace started to say and stopped. "I don't know. I should probably start to think about it."

"What the fuck, Candace?" Danilo said in frustration. "What am I supposed to do now? My father is going to kill me."

Danilo stood up and pulled out his phone. He took a picture.

"What's that for?" she asked.

"Evidence for my father," Danilo said.

"So what's the deal here?" Candace asked. "Are you going to waive your rights or do you want to be involved?"

"My family will take care of you," Danilo said. "They'd never let you put it up for adoption. I told your father that. Man, is he pissed." Danilo chuckled morosely.

"Do you want me to call you when he's born?"

"Sure, text me after he's born." Danilo started to leave and then turned back to her. "No—text me before. My mother will probably want to come."

Then he walked downstairs and let himself out.

Candace rolled onto her side and cradled her belly. "That was your daddy," she whispered.

She logged onto Facebook.

Candy: My baby daddy came to see me today.

Aleecia: Is he going to stay with you?

Candy: No. He hates me. My father confronted him and he came over to yell at me.

Shawna: Maybe it's not always about trying to fix something broken. Maybe it's about starting over and creating something better.

Luciana: My baby daddy is dead. Drug overdose.

Isabella: Mine too. Afghanistan.

Jasmine: Mine should be so lucky!

Sixteen

CANDACE HELPED JULIA SET THE TABLE FOR THANKSGIVING dinner. It was the first week that she had been allowed out of bed and she wore her fleece tracksuit and the bunny slippers Daddy gave her for Christmas the year before. The same Christmas that Danilo had given her the *Garden State* album. *Wow!* she thought, *a lot changes in a year.*

"How many places do we need to set?" Candace yelled toward the kitchen. "Is Daddy coming?"

Sara walked in the front door and dumped her backpack on the front stairs. "Is Daddy coming to what?" she said.

"Thanksgiving. Is Daddy coming?" Candace said.

"God, I hope not." Sara said with bitterness. "I

hate Thanksgiving! What a dumb holiday. Just a stupid meal—and I hate turkey and Brussels sprouts and especially sweet potatoes."

"What is up with you?" Candace asked.

"Tell me you love Thanksgiving," Sara said.

"No, of course not. Anything involving family meals and too much food and discussions of my weight? Please!" Candace said.

Just then, Candace felt her panties get wet.

"Shit, I need to pee!" she said and ran to the bathroom. But it wasn't like regular pee. Water just kept dribbling out and it smelled like the ocean. "Mommy!" she shouted. "Sara? Can anybody hear me? Help!"

"What's up?" Sara said through the door.

"Get Mommy! I think something is happening." Candace heard Sara running upstairs, shouting. There were lots of footsteps pounding on the hardwood floors and then Mommy's voice came through the door.

"Candace, unlock the door! What is happening?"

Candace opened the door. The smell of brine was overwhelming.

"Your water broke," Mommy said. "The baby is coming. Are you feeling contractions?"

"No," Candace said.

"Okay, wash up; I'll call Dr. Bird." Mommy was all business.

Candace had changed her underwear and sat gingerly on a stool in the kitchen. "What did the doctor say?" she asked.

"We need to wait for the contractions to start," Mommy said. "It could be twenty-four hours. If nothing happens by tomorrow, we'll go to the hospital."

"What does that feel like?" Candace asked. "How will I know?"

"Did you not read the book I gave you? It's like a vice around your abdomen. There's nothing to compare it to. You'll know," Mommy said. "Get a towel from the linen closet. I don't want you staining the dining room chair."

And then to Julia, "Is everything ready?"

"Are we expecting Mr. Parker?" Julia asked.

"I'm not sure," Mommy said. "Leave a place set for him and let's start with the salad."

Candace and Sara took their seats and folded their hands in their laps.

"Let's count our blessings," Mommy said. "I'll start. I'm thankful for my health, our beautiful home, and that business has been good this year at the store. Your turn, Sara."

"I'm thankful that my team won regionals," Sara said.

"Candace?" Mommy said.

"I'm thankful that I am out of bed. I'm thankful that the baby is coming and this will be over soon."

"Over?" Mommy said. "Candace, this is just beginning. This isn't like adopting a puppy. You're going to have to feed the baby, change the baby, and bathe the baby. This baby will be your entire life for the next eighteen years. What about college? What about dating? You'll be thirty-six before your life will be your own again."

"Geez, Mommy," said Candace. "I had no idea how you felt about having children."

The front door opened and Daddy walked in.

"George!" Mommy said. "We didn't know you were coming."

"Who did you think was going to carve the turkey?" Daddy walked around the table kissing Sara, then Mommy and then Candace on the head. "Happy Thanksgiving, ladies," Daddy said. He sat at the head of the table and picked up the carving knife and fork.

"George," Mommy said. "Are you drunk?"

"Maybe a little."

Candace had never seen Daddy this way.

"Who wants a wing?" Daddy said.

"I do," said Sara.

"White meat for me, please," said Candace.

As Daddy served up the turkey, Julia passed around heaping bowls of potatoes, spinach, carrots, and squash.

"Before we dig in, let's say grace," Mommy said. "George, what are you thankful for?"

"I'm thankful that my biggest account paid me on time and I can afford this spread." Daddy took a big gulp of red wine.

"Okay, girls," Mommy said. Candace and Sara

loaded their forks and inhaled mouthfuls of turkey, vegetables, and Julia's fresh baked corn bread.

The Parkers ate in silence, savoring the rich food.

"Candace's water broke today so we might be spending the night at the hospital," Mommy said.

"Who's ready for seconds?" Daddy said and hacked away at the carcass.

"Shit!" Blood spurted out of his left thumb.

"George, what did you do?" Mommy said.

Daddy wrapped his hand in a linen napkin and squeezed it to staunch the bleeding.

"Julia, bring a bandage!" Mommy shouted.

Daddy stood over the kitchen sink while Julia wound the gauze five, six times and still the blood flowed.

"Hold your hand over your head," Julia said.

Daddy did as he was told but blood started running down his arm, staining his crisp white shirt.

"Shit!" Daddy said.

"Does it hurt?" Sara asked.

"Like a sonofabitch!" Daddy said. "I think I cut off the end of my thumb."

"Should we call an ambulance?" Candace asked.

"Somebody get me a hand towel," Daddy said. "Lois, call a cab. Shit, shit, shit!"

Daddy held his hand over the sink and changed the towel every few minutes until the cab arrived.

Candace and Sara ran with Daddy to the front door trying to avoid dripping blood on the Persian carpet.

"Bye, Daddy," Sara said. "Will you call us from the hospital?"

Daddy slammed the car door and they heard the cab peel away.

"Well, that was exciting," Mommy said. "Who wants pumpkin pie?"

"I'm stuffed," Candace said. She flopped onto the sofa and Sara sat down beside her.

"I need to lie down," Candace said.

"Still no contractions?" Sara asked.

"Nothing." Candace said. "What does the book say?"

Sara pulled up WebMD on her iPad and searched around.

"Here it is. We're supposed to wait twenty-four

hours and then if nothing happens, we go to the hospital to induce labor," Sara said.

"Induce?" Candace asked. "What's that?"

"They give you drugs to force the contractions," Sara said. "Does that hurt?"

"Geez, I hope not," Candace said.

//

In the morning, Candace went down to the kitchen for breakfast. Julia was making coffee and Mommy was reading the newspaper.

"Anything?" Mommy asked.

"I'm not sure," Candace said. "Maybe I felt some cramps?"

"Honey, you would know," Mommy said. "I'll call Dr. Bird after breakfast. She may want you to come in or she may want to wait until Monday."

"Can I have waffles?" Candace said.

Julia shot her a secret smile and plugged in the waffle iron. "What are we naming the baby?" she said.

"I don't know," Candace said. "Mommy, is there a family name?"

"Well, the Swifts came over on the *Mayflower*. Let's see: Simon, Pierce, Jacob, Jeremiah, these are family names."

Just then, Sara walked in. "How about Walker? We could call him Wally? Or Winston, we could call him Winny."

"Wally, Winny," Candace said. "Gross! What about something Italian, like Lorenzo. We could call him Lorrie?"

"That sounds stupid," Sara said. "What about Mikey? Or Matty?"

"I love the name, Matty! Matthew—no, Matteo Parker," Candace said. "I like that." She caressed her belly. "Hello Matteo."

The baby kicked.

Seventeen

"Oh, I think I felt something," Candace said. "Shouldn't we go to the hospital?"

Mommy dialed Dr. Bird's number and got the answering service.

"Please tell Dr. Bird that Candace's water broke yesterday at three p.m. and she hasn't gone into labor," Mommy said into the phone.

"Candace, why don't you take a shower," Mommy said. "This is going to be a long weekend."

///

Candace was packing her overnight bag with her nightgown and toothbrush when Sara knocked.

"We gotta go," Sara said. "The doctor wants you to go to the hospital."

Candace texted Danilo: baby coming. Tell your mom.

Several minutes went by and then he responded. She's in NY. She'll come tomorrow. Brigham & Women's Hospital?

Candace texted, Yes, but call first. We might be home by tomorrow.

//

Candace lay in the hospital bed, shivering—not from cold, but from nervous anticipation.

"This is it, Matty," she whispered to her belly. "You're coming out whether you like it or not. Please don't hurt me."

A doctor walked in, wearing scrubs and a mask. He pulled down the mask and smiled kindly at Candace. "I'm Dr. Weed, your anesthesiologist. First, we'll relax you a little bit with some gas, and then we'll administer an epidural."

"What's that?" Candace asked. Her teeth were chattering.

"I'll insert a needle into your spine to numb you from the waist down. Then we'll give you oxytocin, which will cause the contractions to start. The epidural will help you tolerate the contractions and let your body do its work. Your doctor will come in to explain what will happen over the course of the next several hours."

"Can my mother and sister come in?" Candace asked.

"Yes, they can be with you the whole time," Dr. Weed said.

"Do you know where they are?" Candace asked.

"I'll ask the nurse to fetch them as soon as we're done here. I want you to take deep breaths into the mask and count backwards from one hundred."

Dr. Weed put the mask over her nose and Candace started to panic.

"I can't breathe!" she said, swatting at Dr. Weed and knocking the mask off her face.

"Okay, Candace." Dr. Weed spoke slowly and calmly. "I'll get the nurse and she'll give you a shot to help you relax."

As Dr. Weed left the room, Candace sat up and scanned the room in a panic. "Where are my clothes?" she said out loud. "We need to get out of here, I need to get out of here, Squirt—I mean, Matty."

Just then Mommy and Sara walked in, accompanied by a nurse.

"Candace, get back into bed!" Mommy snapped. "What do you think you are doing?"

"I'm scared, Mommy," Candace said. "I want to go home."

"Don't be ridiculous!" Mommy said.

The nurse put a hand on Mommy's arm and Mommy shook it off.

"Take your hands off me!" Then to Candace, she said, "You're not going to give us any trouble, young lady. You're going to lie back and obey. The doctor will take care of everything."

The nurse approached Candace and stroked her arm. "I'm Nurse Remy. You can call me Rosie. I'm going to hook you up to an IV. This won't hurt; just a little prick and then you'll start to feel calm and relaxed. Now give me your arm. Make a fist. That's a good girl."

It was over before Candace even noticed. *Rosie is good*, she thought.

Then Rosie turned to Mommy. "Mrs. Parker, would you like a little something to take the edge off, as well?"

Mommy managed a weak smile. "Yes, that would be lovely," she said. "Thank you."

"Let's get you something from the pharmacy."

Mommy followed Rosie out of the room.

When they were gone, Sara stroked Candace's head. "How are you feeling?" she asked.

"Fuzzy," Candace replied.

"That's good," Sara said. "I'm your coach, now. And after that performance I doubt the nurses will let Mommy back in here. Maybe they'll knock her out and she'll leave us alone."

Candace giggled.

"Okay, coach, what does the book say?" Candace said. "Remind me, why do I need an epidural?"

Sara pulled out her iPad. "Let's see." She scanned WebMD. "Epidural anesthesia is the most popular method of pain relief during labor."

"So I won't feel a thing?" Candace said.

"Um, I wouldn't go that far," Sara said, reading again from her iPad. "The goal of an epidural is to provide pain relief, as opposed to anesthesia which leads to a total lack of feeling."

Just then, Dr. Weed walked in. "Ladies, how are we feeling?"

"I'm Sara. I'm the coach."

"Nice to meet you, Sara. How is our patient doing?"

"Fuzzy, she says."

"Fuzzy is good," Dr. Weed said.

"That's what I said," said Sara.

"Candace, are we ready for the next step? I need you to roll on your side and arch your back. You'll feel a little prick—that will be the local anesthesia. Then I'm going to insert a catheter into your spine."

Candace rolled over and felt Dr. Weed wiping her lower back with something cold and wet.

"Ow!" Candace yelped and jerked.

"You need to lie still, Candace. That was the local; we'll give that a minute. This next bit shouldn't pinch as much," Dr. Weed said. "Sara, why don't you stand by Candace's head and hold her hand. Candace, try to lie still and squeeze Sara's hand."

"Ow!" Sara screamed. "You're digging your nails into me!"

"Ladies, we're almost done here," Dr. Weed said. "Everybody stay calm."

Candace felt an uncomfortable pressure on her lower back and bit her lip to resist crying out.

A minute later, Dr. Weed said, "Good job, ladies. We're all set here. Candace, I'll be back in fifteen minutes to check on your progress. Coach, keep an eye on her. The nursing station is right outside if you need anything."

Candace was still clinging to Sara's hand.

"How are you feeling?" Sara asked.

"Weird," Sarah said. "I feel like I can't breathe."

"Stay here, I'll call the nurse."

"Seriously, where would I go?" Candace said. She giggled. "Hey kid, I'm glad you're here with me."

"I *love* being the coach!" Sara said. "Imagine the term paper I could write! Be right back."

Sara scooted out the door.

Sara was back in a flash with Nurse Rosie in tow.

"Candace, how are you doing?" Rosie asked.

"I can't breathe, I feel like I'm suffocating," Candace said, gasping for air.

"I'll get Dr. Weed," Rosie said. "Sara, stay with her."

Dr. Weed walked in and checked the monitor behind Candace's head.

"Let's dial this back and see how you feel," he said. "Give it a minute. How is it now?"

"I still can't feel my lungs," Candace said. She was starting to panic.

"Let's adjust your IV too." Dr. Weed spoke in a low tone to Nurse Remy and she adjusted Candace's sedative.

"How are we doing now?" Dr. Weed asked.

Candace sucked in a large breath and sighed. "Better," she said.

Dr. Bird entered the room. "Candace how are we doing?"

"Fine," Candace said weakly.

"Here's what's going happen next," Dr. Bird said. "We're going to start the oxytocin and you'll start to feel contractions. First five minutes apart, then we'll gradually up the dosage until the frequency increases. Sara, you need to keep track of the contractions—how long they last and how long in between. The most important thing—when you feel a contraction, don't push. Remember your breathing? When you feel a contraction, breathe. If you start pushing before you're fully dilated, you could hurt the baby. I'll be back in forty-five minutes or so to check on your progress."

"Wow, this is really it," said Sara. "Squeeze my hand when the contraction starts and I'll watch the clock. This is exciting!"

Eighteen

THE FIRST CONTRACTION HIT AND CANDACE SCREAMED. The pain started in her lower back and radiated to the front of her rib cage. *Like a vise around your abdomen,* Mommy had said. She felt like she was being ripped open.

"What the fuck!" Candace yelled.

"Can you imagine what you'd be feeling without the epidural?" Sara said, grinning.

"Fuck you!" Candace screamed. "Do you think this is funny?"

"Breathe, whoo, whoo, whoo, whoo, sssssss— remember?" Sara said.

The agony ended. Sara held a cold washcloth to Candace's forehead.

"Who the fuck invented this breathing bullshit?" Candace said. "How, exactly is this helping?"

"Fernand Lamaze," Sara said, reading from her iPad. "Patterned breathing is intended to both increase oxygenation and interfere with the transmission of pain signals from the uterus to the cerebral cortex."

"Let's both just agree that he was an asshole who had no idea what the fuck he was talking about," Candace said.

They laughed until another contraction caught Candace up short.

This time she just screamed, "Eeeeeee," until the pain subsided.

"Screaming definitely works better than breathing," Candace said. "Next time, scream with me."

With the next contraction, Candace squeezed Sara's hand as they both screamed at the top of their lungs.

///

Several hours later, Candace and Sara were both drenched in sweat. Dr. Bird had examined her several times and announced her progress: two centimeters dilated, four centimeters. Candace had been stuck at six centimeters for two hours.

"I can't go on," Candace wailed. "He's not coming out."

Sara pressed a fresh wet cloth to Candace's forehead.

"What are we going to do?" Sara asked.

"I think I'm going to die, right here on this bed," Candace said. "I can't do this anymore, I can't take one more contraction. I think maybe Squirt is already dead."

Sara looked alarmed. "I'm going to call Maria," she said.

"Who's Maria?" Candace said. "I want Rosie."

"Rosie left for the day," Sara said. She pressed the wet cloth to her own forehead. "Maria is the night nurse."

Just then, Candace had an overwhelming need

to poop. "Call Maria! I need to go the bathroom. Now!"

Sara ran out and came running back with Nurse Maria.

"I need to go the bathroom," Candace said. She struggled to sit up.

"All right," Maria said, soothingly. She checked the computer monitor and then stepped to the foot of Candace's bed.

And then suddenly, something moved. Candace had the sensation that her entire insides were about to fall out.

"Something is happening!" Candace bellowed. *Why isn't anybody helping me? I have to go to the bathroom!*

"What is it?" Sara's scared voice came through the door.

Nurse Maria was examining Candace. "You're complete," she said, looking satisfied. "Sara, tell the nursing station to page Dr. Bird."

Sara dashed down the hall. *Complete? What the hell does that mean?* Candace thought.

Moments later, Dr. Bird rushed in. "Let's take a peek." She peered between Candace's legs. "Good girl, Candace. You did it. The baby is ready. I can see the head. Now it's time to push. The next time you feel a contraction I want you to bear down. When the contraction stops, you need to lie back and relax. Sara, help her sit up."

"C'mon, Candace, we practiced this," Sara said.

Candace groaned as she felt the contraction.

"Push!" Sara said.

When it was over, Candace collapsed into the pillow, gasping. "Oh no, here's another one!"

"Push!" Sara yelled.

Dr. Bird peered up over her safety glasses and mask. "Candace, one more push and he'll be out. Make this one count."

"C'mon team, we can do this!" Sara yelled. "PUSH!"

Candace screamed and pushed with what strength she had left. The baby slid out like a seal off of a slippery rock. Candace craned to see him. "Is he okay?"

Dr. Bird fussed with him for a second and then they heard a wail.

"He's crying!" Candace said and burst into tears.

Maria weighed the baby and checked his signs. "Seven pounds, one ounce," she said. Then she bundled him up and set him on Candace's belly. "Hold your baby," she said.

"Oh my God, oh my God," Candace said over and over. "Look at his hair —just as I imagined him. Look at his green eyes!"

Dr. Bird was still fussing around between Candace's legs. "One more push and we'll get the placenta out," she said.

"Gross!" Sara cried.

Candace laughed, tears streaming down her face.

"Where's Mommy?" Candace asked.

"She's resting in the lounge," Maria said. "I'll get her."

Sara pulled out her iPhone and started taking pictures.

"Oh my God, I must look hideous!" Candace said.

"Yeah, you do," Sara said.

"Fuck you," Candace said. "You look like shit, too! Let me take your picture. Here, hold Matty." She handed the baby to Sara, gingerly. "Hold his head!"

"I got it!" Sara said. "I was the coach and now I'm the aunt. I am going to spoil this little guy."

Candace was snapping photos when Mommy walked in.

"Mommy, take one of all three of us," Sara said. She handed Matty back to Candace and perched on the bed beside them.

Mommy dug her phone out of her purse. "Well, Candace, you did it. You're a mother now."

"Right, we can't call you Mommy anymore," Sara said. "We have to call you Grand-mommy. How about Grommy?" Candace and Sara guffawed.

"It's pronounced Grammy, I think." Mommy said. "What about Danilo's family? Are they coming to claim their grandson?"

"His mother is coming tomorrow," Candace said.

"Tomorrow, you'll be at home," Mommy said. "They are discharging you at ten a.m."

"Then I guess she'll come to the house," Candace said.

"The house?" Mommy said. "Good God, we need time to prepare. Sara, let's go."

"Mommy, I'm tired," Sara said. "I don't want to clean my room tonight."

"She's not going to see your room!" Candace said.

"Enough!" Mommy said. "Sara, let's go."

Maria walked in. "We're going take Matteo for a few tests and we'll bring his bassinet to your room." She took the baby from Candace. "You need to rest now and get ready to breastfeed him. Visitors out."

"Okay, Maria," Candace said. "Thank you."

Sara gave Candace a big hug. "Bye. See you tomorrow."

"Love you," Candace said.

"Me too," Sara said.

"We'll see you in the morning," Mommy said. "We'll meet you downstairs."

Candace jolted awake when Maria entered the room in a flood of light from the hallway.

"Here we are," Maria said in a soft voice. "Mr. Matteo is hungry." She wheeled the basinet up next to the bed. "Sit up, honey, and I'll plump up your pillows."

Candace sat up and started shivering again. "What do I do? How does this work?"

"Don't worry, Candace, I'm an expert," Maria said. "Just relax and let your body do its job."

Maria handed the baby to Candace and showed her how to cradle his head near her nipple. Matteo's mouth gaped like a baby bird.

"Ooh, he's hungry," Maria said. "Squeeze your breast a little and let him take the nipple."

"Ow," Candace whispered. "He's biting me, gumming me, I mean."

"Take slow, deep breaths. It'll help you relax and help your milk flow," Maria said. "Look what a good job you're doing. A lot of moms have trouble with breastfeeding. I'll leave you two alone. When he's done, be sure to burp him—they showed you that in class, right? Hold him up on your shoulder and rub his back until he burps."

"Yes," Candace whispered. "We practiced with a baby doll."

"Good girl. After he burps, try the other breast and see if he'll take a little more. I'll be back in a few minutes to check on you." Maria slipped out the door.

Nineteen

"I CAN'T BELIEVE YOU'RE HERE," CANDACE WHISPERED, stoking Matty's head. "Wait until Daddy sees you. He'll change his mind and come back home."

Matteo nodded off and dropped her nipple.

"C'mon, baby," Candace said. "We need to burp." She held Matteo up to her left shoulder and rubbed his back until he belched and spit up on her gown.

"Yikes," Candace said. "That was gross!" She cradled Matteo under her right breast and he latched on, nursing hungrily. She burped him one more time.

Maria poked her head in the door. "How are you doing?"

"I think he's asleep," Candace said. "I burped him and he barfed all over me."

Maria laughed. "Let me put him to bed. I'll get you a fresh gown and then you should try to get some sleep. He'll need to nurse again in an hour or two."

"He eats every hour?" Candace said.

"When they are little, they do" Maria said. "As they grow, they can go longer between feedings, maybe two hours at a time, then three and so on."

"How will I know when he needs to eat again?" Candace asked.

"Oh, don't worry, he'll let you know." Maria chuckled as she laid Matteo in the basinet.

Between nurses barging into her room to check on her and Matteo needing to nurse, Candace got very little sleep that night. And then it was time to go home. Nurse Rosie wheeled Candace down the hall to the front entrance where Mommy and Sara were waiting.

"Can I hold him?" Sara was jumping up and down on the sidewalk.

"Be careful," Candace said. "Do you know how to work the car seat?"

Candace sat in the back seat of the car with Matteo and Mommy drove them home.

"Have you heard from Mrs. Rossi?" Mommy asked.

"She is supposed to be coming by the house at around three this afternoon," Candace said.

Mommy didn't say anything, but Candace saw that she was gripping the steering wheel so hard that her knuckles were white. Candace put on her headphones and slumped down the seat.

///

At two fifty-six, the doorbell rang. Candace and Sara sat stiffly on the sofa. Mommy sat in a side chair nursing a glass of red wine. Baby Matteo was upstairs, sleeping.

"Julia," Mommy said. "Could you get the door?"

Julia opened the door. "Good afternoon, Mrs. Rossi, Mr. Danilo."

Mommy stood as Danilo and his mother entered

the room. She was tall and sleek, impeccably dressed in designer knits in hues of gold and rust.

"Hello, Mrs. Rossi," Mommy said.

"Call me Filomena," Mrs. Rossi said.

"Lois," Mommy said, touching her chest. "I'd like to introduce my daughters, Candace and Sara."

Filomena nodded in their direction.

"Would you like to sit down?" Mommy said. "Can I get you something to drink?"

Filomena looked at Mommy's glass and said, "Whatever you're having."

"Julia, why don't you bring the bottle?" Mommy said. "And bring a soda for Danilo."

Filomena sat opposite Mommy and Danilo squeezed in next to Sara on the sofa.

"You will have the child baptized?" Filomena asked.

"Baptized?" Mommy said.

"You're not Catholic?" Filomena asked.

"Unitarian," Mommy replied.

"What is that?" Filomena asked. "No, never mind. Can we see the child? Matteo is his name?"

"Julia, can you bring the baby down?" Mommy said.

"He's sleeping, Mommy," said Candace.

Filomena looked at Candace for the first time. "We can't stay long."

Julia brought the baby down and handed him to Candace.

Candace stood and walked over to Filomena's chair. "Would you like to hold him?"

Filomena gazed at Matteo and her face softened. "He looks exactly like Danilo did as a baby," she said. She touched the baby's face but made no move to take him from Candace's arms. "He is a Rossi. That is the name on the birth certificate—yes?"

"Yes," Candace replied, softly. "We thought it would be best."

"Yes," Filomena said softly. "That's best. And when he is older he can come to Italy and meet his cousins." Filomena looked Candace in the eye. "Danilo is a young and irresponsible boy. This is not the way we raised him. He is a disgrace to the Rossi name."

Candace glanced over at Danilo. He was sweating and squirming in his chair.

Lois interrupted, "That's not the way Candace was raised either. She is supposed to be studying at Princeton right now."

"Candace seems like a responsible young woman to me," Filomena said. "What would you have her do? Abort the child? That's unheard of. No, she will raise the child, but we take care of our own. The baby needs to know his father's family too. Here's what we're prepared to do. We will wire you a lump sum of two thousand euros each month until the child is eighteen. Danilo will work out the details." Filomena drained her glass and rose.

"Very nice to meet you," Filomena said to Mommy. She touched Candace's shoulder. "Take care of my grandson."

Candace smiled nervously and nodded.

"Danilo, get the door," Filomena commanded.

Danilo jumped up. He didn't look at Candace.

"Goodbye," Sara said.

Julia shut the door behind them.

"Did you see what she was wearing?" Sara said. "Mommy, you need to carry that designer in your shop! *Tres* elegant."

"That's French," Candace said.

"How do you say it in Italian?" Sara said.

"Two thousand euros," Mommy said. "You can't live on that. What is your plan?"

"I've been thinking." Candace gently rocked the baby in her arms. "What if I live here and enroll at UMass Boston? Julia and Sara can help out, right?"

"Sure!" Sara said.

"Of course," Julia said.

"We'll make it work, Mommy, we will," said Candace. "And two thousand euros, that's not nothing. That will pay for food and clothes and diapers."

"And your food, and your clothes and your tuition?" Mommy said. "Who will pay for that?"

"I'll get a job," Candace said.

"Me, too," Sara said.

Matteo woke up and started to wail.

"I think he's hungry again," Candace said. "C'mon baby, let's go upstairs."

Once Matty was asleep, Candace logged onto Facebook. She had posted Sara and Mommy's hospital photos on her feed, plus a photo of Matteo sleeping.

Luci: He's gorgeous!

Candy: He wakes up every two hours to eat. I'm exhausted.

Jasmine: It gets easier. Eventually they sleep 6 hours and you can take a real nap.

Candy: The good news is that I'm skinnier now! My maternity jeans are too big for me.

Shawna: Keep it up—breastfeeding is God's natural method of birth control and weight loss.

Aleecia: Oh man I hope so. I've gained 80 pounds already.

Jasmine: You've got to eat healthy. And exercise every day. I need to get back in shape fast so I can audition.

Isabella: Audition for what?

Jasmine: I'm a dancer. It's what I do for a living.

Twenty

ON CHRISTMAS EVE, CANDACE DRESSED MATTEO LIKE A candy cane in a red-and-white-striped onesie and matching hat that she had found online. She strapped him into his BabyBjorn and carried him down to the living room where Mommy sat on the floor, surrounded by boxes of ornaments and decorations that Julia had dragged down from the attic. Christmas carols played softly in the background.

I love Christmas, Candace thought.

"You could put him down, every now and then," Mommy said.

"I don't mind carrying him, and it keeps him happy," Candace said.

"He needs to learn to be alone and comfort himself," Mommy said.

"He's only four weeks old," Candace said, "He has plenty of time to figure out how to be alone." She stood with her back to the fireplace, savoring the warmth.

"Not so close to the fire," Mommy said. "You'll scorch him."

Candace retreated to the couch and surveyed the familiar holiday tableau.

Sara came down the stairs. "We're doing the tree? Why didn't you call me? I call tinsel!"

"No tinsel for you," Mommy said. "Help me with the lights."

"Is Daddy coming for dinner?" Sara asked.

"I don't know," Mommy said. "I hope so. I invited Danilo too."

"Why would you invite Danilo?" Candace said, alarmed.

"I thought we could try to negotiate peace in the family," Mommy said. She had tears in her eyes. "He can't stay away forever."

"Danilo isn't going to make it better," Candace said. "He's only going to make everything worse."

"I don't think he's coming, anyway," said Mommy. "I think he went to Rome for Christmas."

"Are you in touch with him?" Candace said.

"I saw it on your Facebook feed," Mommy said.

"If Daddy comes over, don't let him near the carving knives," Sara said, laughing.

Mommy sighed. "I asked Julia to slice the roast before she brings it out."

"You're snooping on my Facebook?" Candace asked, indignant.

"Isn't that what it's for?" Mommy said. "Sharing? You have all of Matteo's baby photos up there. What do your friends say?"

"To my face, or behind my back?" Candace said. "I think they feel sorry for me. Like something awful happened to me. Nobody called me to invite me to brunch over winter break. Anyway, I have new friends."

"New friends?" Mommy said.

"Her teen-mom friends," Sara said. "It's a Facebook group."

"There's a group for that?" Mommy asked.

"There's a group for everything," Sara said.

"Well, that's nice," Mommy said. "Do they live in Brookline?"

"Uh, no," said Sara. "St. Louis, Las Vegas, California, Florida. All over the place."

"Geez," Candace said. "Is everybody snooping on my Facebook?"

"It's not snooping," Sara said. "It's sharing. Right, Mommy?"

Sara placed the last ornament on the tree. "Time for tinsel! Mommy, please?"

Matteo started to whimper. "Hey, Aunt Sara," Candace said. "Do you want to change Matty?"

"Sure!" Sara said. "C'mon, baby."

Candace unsnapped the BabyBjorn and handed Matteo over to Sara.

"Whoa!" Sara said. "Stinky!" She held him at arm's length. "C'mon, stinkmeister!"

"Could you not call him that?" Candace said laughing. "Only I get to call him that."

Sara carried the baby upstairs.

"C'mon, Mommy," Candace said conspiratorially. "She's gone—let's finish the tree."

When Sara came back downstairs, the tree was trimmed and the boxes were piled in a corner. Mommy switched on the lights.

"Wow!" Sara said. "Look Matty, how pretty! Where are the presents? Can we pile presents under the tree?"

"There's something about having a baby in the house that makes Christmas so much more fun," Mommy said. "Not that I would ever have wished this on you or any of us. We could have waited another ten years."

Candace took Matteo from Sara. "Look in my closet," Candace said. "And the hall closet. And Mommy's closet—right, Mommy? You always hid our presents in your closet. Not such a great hiding place."

Sara dashed up and down the stairs carrying

armloads of wrapped boxes and positioned them carefully under the tree. When she was done, she stepped back. "It looks great! Good job, Team Parker!"

"I applied to UMass," Candace said quietly.

"You did?" Mommy asked.

"Biology," Candace said. "I should hear something in March."

"Why Biology?" Sara asked.

"I think I'd like to go to med school," Candace said. "Someday. I'd like to be an OB-GYN. Maybe specialize in teen pregnancies."

"Don't tell your father," Mommy said. "Let's try to have a nice Christmas dinner."

//

Sara was carting boxes down to the basement and Julia was whipping up her signature eggnog when the doorbell rang.

Candace opened the door with Matteo strapped to her chest.

"Daddy!" Sara shouted. "Come look at the tree."

Sara escorted Daddy into the living room. "Very nice, girls," he said.

"Would you like a cocktail?" Mommy called from the kitchen.

"Bourbon, please," said Daddy.

Mommy carried a glass of brown liquid to Daddy. "Neat?" she asked. He took the glass. She kissed him, hard, on the lips. "Please come home."

"I'll stay tonight," he said. Then he took a sip of his drink.

"Dinner is served," Julia said.

"I love Christmas," Sara said. "So much better than Thanksgiving. Roast beef, mashed potatoes, green beans and French rolls. Why can't we have this for Thanksgiving too?"

"At my house," Candace said, "this will be what we have for Thanksgiving."

"Then I'm coming to your house," Sara said.

"Your house?" Daddy said. "Where is that?"

"When I get out of college, I mean," Candace said.

"College?" Daddy said. "When are you going to college?"

"George, Candace, please," said Mommy. "It's Christmas."

"Two thousand euros a month." Daddy said. "What can you afford on that?"

"Julia, the meal is exquisite," Mommy said. "Why don't you go home and spend the holiday with your family? There's an envelope in the foyer for you. Merry Christmas."

"Thank you, Mrs. P," Julia said. "Merry Christmas."

"Merry Christmas!" Candace and Sara chimed in.

"George," Mommy said, "You're home with us. Can we just have a nice evening?"

"Why did I spend two hundred thousand dollars on that fucking private school?" Daddy said. "For what? What is your plan Candace?"

"I applied to UMass," Candace said. "They have a good Biology program."

"Candace!" Mommy said. "I asked you not to."

"UMass?" Daddy said. "Well, sure they do. But I didn't need to take out a second mortgage for you to get into UMass. What about that, Candace?"

Matteo wailed from upstairs.

"I gotta go," Candace said. "Thank you for dinner, Mommy. It was delicious."

"Of course you have to go!" Daddy yelled after her.

"Candace!" Mommy yelled. "Don't forget the presents. Let's open presents tonight."

//

Christmas morning arrived. Matteo woke the Parker household up with his hungry wail. Sara tiptoed downstairs and turned on the tree lights. She threw some logs in the fireplace and lit a match. Candace came down when she smelled the coffee brewing.

"Where are Mommy and Daddy?" Candace whispered.

"I don't know." Sara said. "Should I make waffles?"

"Please," Candace said. "With strawberries and whipped cream, right baby?" She kissed Matteo's head. He was snug in his BabyBjorn. "Oh, you smell so nice, I could gobble you up."

Mommy came downstairs to find the girls sitting in front of the fireplace with a breakfast picnic spread out on a blanket: waffles and eggs, coffee and juice. Matteo lay on his back on a baby blanket next to Candace.

"Merry Christmas, Mommy," Candace said. "Can we fix you a plate?"

"That would be lovely," Mommy said. "Make one for Daddy too. He'll be down in a minute."

Candace and Sarah gaped at each other and simultaneously mouthed the words, "Daddy is back!"

Twenty one

"HOW IS THE JOB SEARCH GOING?" DADDY ASKED ONE morning at breakfast.

"I've applied everywhere: Starbucks, Pete's Coffee, Citibank, Star Market, Walgreens, Children's Place, Stop & Shop, Subway, Lord & Taylor and Macy's," Candace said. "I'm going to ride in with Mommy today and try all the stores in Back Bay."

"My friend's mom is a chef," Sara said. "She has a couple of restaurants—one in Cambridge and one in Seaport. Do you want me to ask him to ask his mom?"

"Please," Candace said. "I'll do anything. Wash dishes, take out the trash, coat check, anything."

Candace arrived for the interview in a new Kenneth Cole outfit she had found at Lord & Taylor: slim black pants and a white flowing blouse. Julia had tied her hair back in a French braid. She felt like a million bucks.

The hostess asked her to wait at a table near the window. She caught her reflection and thought, *I look so grown-up. Not like some teen-mom, drop-out loser.*

"Hello, I'm Felix."

He was tall and dark-skinned, with long wavy hair. *Probably gay,* Candace thought. He sat down at the table opposite her.

"Your mom is a friend of Jody?" Felix asked.

Candace had no idea who Jody was. "No, my sister's friend knows somebody who works here. Somebody's mom or something."

"I see," Felix said. "Well, we can start you out in coat check. And depending on how that goes, maybe move you up to hostess."

"That would be great!" Candace said.

"You're available full-time?" Felix asked. "We're not interested in hiring people who are going to leave to go back to school in the fall."

"I'm not in school," Candace said.

"The hours are four p.m. to ten p.m., Tuesday through Thursday," Felix said. "Midnight on Friday and Saturday."

"Four to twelve on Friday and Saturday?" Candace asked.

"Yes," Felix said. "Is that a problem?"

Candace thought about Matty. How would she feed him and put him to bed?

"No," she said. "No problem."

"What you're wearing right now is fine," Felix said. "Black pants and white blouse and shoes with a low heel, minimal jewelry—that's the uniform. Do you have a few more ensembles like that in your closet?"

Ensembles? Definitely gay, Candace thought. "Sure. No problem," she said.

"Can you start tomorrow?" Felix said. "Be here at three-thirty."

Candace stood up and shook his hand. "Thank you."

"Wear your hair down, honey," Felix said. "And bare a little cleavage—sexy but tasteful. You'll earn better tips."

On the T home, she worked over in her head how this would work. *Matty wakes up at six. I'll feed him and bathe him and Sara can watch him while I shower. Sara leaves for school at eight. I'll feed him right before I leave for work at two-thirty and Julia can watch him until Sara comes home at six. I'll leave a couple of bottles of breast milk in the fridge. Then I can feed him when I get back at ten-thirty. Except on weekends. Sara will have to feed him and put him to bed on weekends.*

Candace got off at Copley and walked to Lord & Taylor to pick up a few more "ensembles."

//

At dinner that night, Candace broached the subject.

"In other news. . ." Candace said.

Mommy put down her fork. "What is it this time?" she said.

"I got a job," Candace said. "I'm working at Tirade—the restaurant on Pacific Avenue? It's nine dollars an hour plus tips. I'm working three-thirty to ten, Tuesday through Thursday and until midnight on Friday and Saturday. That's like three hundred dollars a week, plus tips."

"A waitress?" Daddy asked. "This is what we sent you to St Paul's for?"

"Coat check, actually," Candace said. "Just until I start school in the fall. I'll figure something else out in the fall."

"Imagine if you didn't have your sister and Julia to help out," Mommy said. "How would you manage?"

"I can't even imagine," Candace said. "I'm having a hard time thinking about leaving Matty every night. I'm so grateful for my family, for Sara and Julia. But I'd much rather be here with him than checking coats for snooty rich people."

"Three hundred dollars a week," Sara said. "That's less than half of what the Rossis pay in child support. Is it worth it?"

"Probably not," Candace said. She started to cry. "But I said I'd get a job. I don't want to be a total freeloader. I spent six hundred dollars at Lord & Taylor today on work clothes."

Mommy gasped. "On my charge card?" she said.

"I'll pay the bill," Candace said. "I have the Rossi money."

"This is probably a good thing," Daddy said. "You need to learn what hard work and sacrifice feel like. You should also pay Sara and Julia for their time. What does a babysitter make? I'm thinking ten dollars an hour. Let's see, you make nine dollars an hour as a coat check girl and you pay Sara and Julia ten an hour. Plus tips but subtract taxes. I don't see how the math works on this."

"You don't have to pay me," Sara said. "Matty is my baby, too. And Julia is on salary."

"No, Daddy is right," Candace said. "This means extra work for Julia. I need to pay her something.

But can I just say for the record—you are the best little sister ever!"

Matty started to wail. Candace pushed back from the table.

"You've barely touched your dinner," Mommy said. "You're so thin."

"I never thought I'd hear those words," Candace said. "Ask Julia to keep a plate warm in the oven for me. I'll try to eat something later."

///

Candace clocked in at three-thirty the next day, eager to start a new phase of life—responsible working parent. Felix showed her the locker room, had her fill out some HR paperwork, issued her a time card and name tag and showed her how to register on Zoomshift, the shift-management app. Then he walked her through the kitchen and introduced her to the staff.

"It's pretty easy," Felix said as he showed Candace

the coatroom. "Take personal items, keep track of everything with these numbered tags. Make sure everybody goes home with their own stuff. If anything is left at the end of your shift, document it and leave a note with the hostess in case somebody calls the next day. Lock up before you leave and hand the key to the shift manager. Then clock out. If we have a light night, we may send you home early or ask you not to come in at all. Always check Zoomshift to confirm your shift before you come to work. That will save you some aggravation. The shift manager will update the app by three p.m. Your shift starts at four but you must always clock in by three-fifty. The kitchen opens at five, so for the first hour you'll report to the hostess and help with menu updates and any other task she assigns you. Remember, you're in training for her job, and her evaluation of you will be weighted heavily. Here's the tip jar—you keep all of your own tips and are responsible for reporting them for tax purposes. Just empty the jar at the end of your shift. Tipping is not obligatory but generally our patrons will leave a dollar per item. Never ask for a tip or argue with a patron. Be gracious and attentive. Got it, kid?"

"Check Zoomshift at three p.m. to make sure I'm supposed to come in." Candace ticked the list off on her fingers. "Clock in at three-fifty. Report to the hostess and help her with anything she needs. Unlock the coatroom at five. Keep track of everything in the coatroom and make sure everyone leaves with their own stuff. Lock up at the end of my shift and hand the key to the manager. Report any leftover items to the hostess. I think I've got it."

Felix led Candace to the hostess station. "Marcie, Geoff—this is Candace, our new coat check girl." To Candace he said, "Marcie is the head hostess tonight and Geoff is your shift manager."

"Honey, you've got a little stain on your pretty blouse," Marcie said. "Why don't you go and try to rinse that out?"

Candace looked down and gasped. Her left breast was leaking.

Twenty-two

CANDACE RAN TO THE LOCKER ROOM AND DABBED AT HER new blouse with a paper towel. A waitress walked in and stowed her belongings in a locker. Then she joined Candace at the sink to check her makeup. She had olive skin, tawny, almond-shaped eyes and exotic wavy hair. Candace read her name tag in the mirror: Toni.

"Oh, honey," Toni said. "You have a baby at home?"

"Yes," Candace said. "This has never happened before."

"You need to buy some nursing pads to put in your bra," Toni said. "Here, let's try some paper towels. Take off your blouse. We'll rinse it and blow it dry."

"I'm so embarrassed!" Candace cried.

"Don't be, hon," Toni said. "We've all been there."

"You have a baby?" Candace asked.

"Honey, I got two kids and a deadbeat ex," Toni said. "I'm working two jobs to pay the bills. My mom watches the boys when I work nights."

"My sister is watching my baby," Candace said.

"What about your mom?" Toni asked.

"My mom has her own business," Candace said. "My parents didn't really sign on for this."

"Whose do?" Toni said. "My mom didn't want me to be a single mom. Nobody does. But moms show up to take care of the kids. That's what they're supposed to do."

"My mom isn't really into kids," Candace said.

"Oh, one of those," Toni said. "I get it. Here honey, your blouse is all dry."

"I'd better get back to the coat check," Candace said. She buttoned her blouse.

"You got lucky," Toni said. "Jody, Felix—these are good people. They will take care of you. Do a good job, look after the customers, and you'll be fine. You can work here until your baby is out of college."

Work here until Matty is out of college? Candace blanched at the thought. *Will I end up like Toni—a single mom in my thirties working two jobs? No, not me! I'm going to medical school and become a doctor. I'm going to have a big house in Brookline and a nanny. I'm going to be the most successful teen mom ever. I'll show them!*

//

The first few hours went well. *Coat check is easy,* Candace thought. *Just like Felix said. Take the coat or bag, hang it on a hanger, hand them a numbered ticket. Plenty of time to check email and Facebook.* The customers were generous. She eyed the tip jar. *There must be fifty dollars in there.*

But around six o'clock, Candace started to feel feverish. Her breasts ached; they were hot and swollen. She needed to sit down. She saw Felix across the room and waved at him.

"How you doing, kid?" Felix said.

"I need to pee," Candace said.

"No problem, Geoff will spot you," Felix said. "Did I forget to tell you that? If you need a bathroom break, flag Geoff."

Felix signaled to Geoff and he trotted over.

"Yeah, boss?" Geoff said.

"Spot Candace while she takes a bio break," Felix said.

"Thank you," Candace said and scooted past them, praying she wouldn't bump into anything. Her breasts were on fire.

"Ow, ow, ow," Candace moaned. She sat on the toilet trying to express some milk. Nothing came out.

As her shift wore on, the pain intensified. Her breasts felt like boulders. It seemed as if ten o'clock would never come. Around nine-thirty, Felix appeared at the coat check door and said, "You can clock out, Parker." He eyed the tip jar. "Good first day—the customers seem to like you. Reservations are a little light tomorrow. Be sure to check Zoom before you head in."

As she waited for the T at South Station, Candace thought, *This is too hard! I have to get up and do this again tomorrow? How do single moms do it?* She prayed, *Dear God, please cancel my shift tomorrow. Please? And where is the fucking T? I want to go home!*

//

When Candace walked in the door, Matty was wailing. Candace ran up to her room to find Sara pacing frantically.

"He wouldn't take the bottle," Sara said. "He's so mad at me!"

Candace tore off her blouse and cradled Matty to her breast. "C'mon baby, Mama's here."

Matty latched onto the nipple but got frustrated when nothing came out. He started to wail again.

"Shit!" Candace said. "Please tell me this isn't happening."

"I read that nursing mothers drink wine to relax," Sara said, trying to be helpful.

"Go!" Candace said.

Sara ran down and found an opened bottle of red wine in the cabinet. She grabbed a juice glass and ran back upstairs with the bottle.

"Here, drink this," Sara said, pouring a glass and shoving it at Candace.

Candace took a long swallow and let out a big sigh. "Okay, Matteo, let's try this again." Matty latched on and started to nurse fiercely.

Sara sat down on the bed, gently. "How was work?" she asked.

"Where's Mommy?" Candace said. "Did she leave you here alone with a screaming baby?"

"They went out," Sara said. "To the theater, I think. They said they'd be back around eleven."

"I had no idea how hard this was going to be," Candace said. "My milk was leaking all over my blouse and then my boobs started to swell up and ache. It was horrible! I'm scared that my milk will dry up and he'll starve."

"What are we going to do?" Sara asked.

"We'll start him on formula tomorrow," Candace said. "He needs to get used to drinking from the bottle, and I can't count on my milk supply. I'll nurse him as long as I can, but he needs more."

Matty calmed down and Candace started to relax.

"So, how was work?" Sara asked again.

"Not bad. The people are really nice," Candace said. "This waitress, Toni, she's a single mom too. Oh, and I made seventy-two dollars in tips." Candace pulled a wad of singles out of her pocket and handed it to Sara. "This is for you."

Sara took the cash and meticulously straightened and smoothed the bills into a tidy pile on the bed. "Cool," she said.

"You earned it," Candace said. "Let's go to Walgreens in the morning and buy some formula. Will you do the research? Find out what kind of formula is best at his age—what do the best doctors recommend?"

Sara ran to get her iPad.

"Not now, dummy!" Candace yelled after her. "We can do it in the morning."

//

Eventually, Matty fell asleep. Candace set him down in his crib, gingerly, so as not to wake him. She took her soiled blouse, washed it in the bathroom sink with Woolite and hung it in the shower to dry. She was startled by a commotion downstairs and tiptoed into the hallway to listen.

"George, I was hoping to mend some fences," Mommy was saying.

"Fences?" Daddy asked.

"This is our daughter. Matteo is our grandson," Mommy said. "I know it's not the future you had envisioned for Candace. But think of how much you save on tuition. UMass isn't so bad."

"Really, Lois?" Daddy shouted. "You too? You think this is just about money? It's not about the legacy of the Swift family?"

"Legacy?" Mommy asked.

"Your father never thought I was good enough for you," Daddy said. "Granted, the Parkers didn't come over on the Mayflower. They may have traveled in steerage a few decades later. But, I've worked so hard to give you a house he would be proud of and to send our daughter to a school that even he would never have been admitted to. After twenty-five years of striving, well . . . shit. Why don't I just sell my business and buy a Winnebago? Why don't we just adopt a dog and take to the open road?"

"George, I had no idea you wanted to travel," Mommy said.

The rest of the conversation was muffled as they shut the bedroom door behind them.

Candace smiled. *Things seem so much better than they were a year ago. Matty is amazing—my beautiful little Squirt. Mommy and Daddy are back together. Sara is my rock. I got a job—sure it's hard but I'm lucky. Other people have it so much worse.*

Twenty-three

CANDACE FOUND THE ENVELOPE LYING IN THE FRONT HALL under the mail slot. *Congratulations!* was printed on the outside. She turned it over in her hands, not quite ready to open it, not quite sure how she felt. *Hooray, I got into UMass,* she thought glumly. She remembered how excited she had been to get the letter from Princeton. This was such a different sensation. She had become a different person. She looked at starting school in the fall the way she looked at going to work every day—not with dread, exactly—it was okay—but she'd really rather be home playing with her baby boy. Whenever Candace entered the room, Matty greeted her with a big gummy grin. She was madly in love with him.

He is such a charmer. *Just like his dad,* she thought, ruefully. *How could I have been so dumb? So naïve? What will I tell Matty when he asks about his father? Sure, Danilo's family wanted to have a relationship with their grandson—but what about Danilo? Maybe not?* That thought made her very sad. *I brought a child into the world whose father doesn't want him. What will that do to his psyche? How can I protect him from all the hurt that will come his way? Fuck Danilo. He's the one losing out, here.*

//

At breakfast the next day, Candace rocked Matty in his baby seat with one hand and held her fork with the other. Sara walked in and poured herself a bowl of granola.

"Hey, guess what?" Candace said. "I got into UMass. We can commute together. Yay."

Sara didn't say anything. She went to the fridge and opened a carton of low-fat milk.

"Hello?" Candace said. "Aren't you happy?"

Sara poured milk over her cereal and stirred it with a spoon.

"What's going on?" Candace asked.

Sara sat down at the table and gave her cereal a couple more stirs. Then she put her spoon down on the table and looked Candace in the eye.

"Daddy said I can apply to Ithaca," she said. "He said he can afford to send *one* of us a private university."

Candace felt a pang of envy. "Wow," she said. She was stunned. *Where I used to be the chosen one, now Sara was Daddy's favorite? The world had tilted on its axis.* "We'll miss you—me and Matty." And then realizing how selfish that sounded, she said, "No, really, that's great. Do you want me to help with your applications?"

Sara's face lit up. "That would be great! Thanks!" She jumped up and gave Candace a hug. "I was hoping you'd be happy for me."

"Of course I'm happy for you," Candace said. "Where else are you thinking of applying?"

"My basketball coach said I might be able to play for UConn or Stanford, but I really don't want to play Division I. I would spend all of my time traveling. I would miss a lot of class and have to take my tests on planes and buses. I'd rather play Division III so I could have a fairly normal social life. So I was thinking Tufts or Oberlin. But my dream is to be a coach and a trainer so I need a good phys ed/physiology program—that's why Ithaca would be my first choice."

Candace had stopped listening. When Sara left for college, Matteo would be going on two—he would already be talking and walking. She tried to imagine her life as a single mom: dropping Matty at daycare, riding the bus to UMass, working a part-time job— somewhere near campus, she guessed. What about dating? Mommy's words echoed inside her head. *You'll be thirty-six before your life will be your own again.* Sara had her whole life ahead of her. *Look how excited Sara is,* Candace thought. *Where would I be right now if Matteo had never been born? What would I be doing?* She tried to imagine what spring felt like on the Princeton campus, walking to class with her dorm-mates, studying late into the night in the library. *Prepping for midterms, right about now,* she guessed.

What if she had given Matty up for adoption? She would probably just be recovering from the postpartum hormonal adjustment and struggling to lose the baby weight. She'd be wondering what her son was doing—in whose arms was he snuggling, who was he greeting with those sweet smiles? She couldn't bear the thought of not being with him every waking moment and watching him develop and change before her eyes.

And the pregnancy had been good to her. She was finally the skinny girl of her dreams. Having shed her baby weight plus that pesky twenty pounds, her thighs no longer rubbed together. Instead, now she had become the annoying lady with the stroller who made everyone on the bus wait until she had boarded and then blocked the aisle.

Gazing at Matteo, her wild child, with those crazy curls, humongous green eyes and goofy grin, she thought ahead to all the years of skinned knees and snotty noses, Little League games, and scout meetings. What about soccer? She supposed Danilo had played soccer—she just assumed every kid in Italy played soccer.

She would teach her son to say please and thank you, how to dance and sing, how to ride a bike. And later, how to drive. There would be tears and laughter, crushes and breakups, triumphs and defeats. Then the ultimate heartbreak would come when her little boy would leave her and go off to live a life of youthful freedom and independence that she would never know.